# Confusion in Cleethorpes

*A Sanford 3rd Age Club Mystery (#22)*

David W Robinson

www.darkstroke.com

Copyright © 2021 by David W Robinson
Cover Photography by Adobe Stock © DiViArts
Design by soqoqo
All rights reserved.

No part of this book may be used or reproduced in any manner whatsoever without written permission of the author or Crooked Cat/darkstroke except for brief quotations used for promotion or in reviews. This is a work of fiction. Names, characters, and incidents are used fictitiously.

*First Dark Edition, darkstroke, Crooked Cat Books 2021*

Discover us online:
**www.darkstroke.com**

Find us on instagram:
**www.instagram.com/darkstrokebooks**

Include **#darkstroke** in a photo of yourself holding this book on Instagram and **something nice will happen.**

## About the Author

David Robinson is a Yorkshireman now living in Manchester. Driven by a huge, cynical sense of humour, he's been a writer for over thirty years having begun with magazine articles before moving on to novels and TV scripts.

He has little to do with his life other than write, as a consequence of which his output is prodigious. Thankfully most of it is never seen by the great reading public of the world.

He has worked closely with Crooked Cat Books and darkstroke since 2012, when The Filey Connection, the very first Sanford 3rd Age Club Mystery, was published.

Describing himself as the Doyen of Domestic Disasters he can be found blogging at **www.dwrob.com** and he appears frequently on video (written, produced and starring himself) dispensing his mocking humour at **www.youtube.com/user/Dwrob96/videos**

# The STAC Mystery series:

#1 The Filey Connection
#2 The I-Spy Murders
#3 A Halloween Homicide
#4 A Murder for Christmas
#5 Murder at the Murder Mystery Weekend
#6 My Deadly Valentine
#7 The Chocolate Egg Murders
#8 The Summer Wedding Murder
#9 Costa del Murder
#10 Christmas Crackers
#11 Death in Distribution
#12 A Killing in the Family
#13 A Theatrical Murder
#14 Trial by Fire
#15 Peril in Palmanova
#16 The Squire's Lodge Murders
#17 Murder at the Treasure Hunt
#18 A Cornish Killing
#19 Merry Murders Everyone
#20 A Tangle in Tenerife
#21 Tis The Season To Be Murdered
#22 Confusion in Cleethorpes
#23 Murder on the Movie Set

Tales from the Lazy Luncheonette Casebook

## By the same author:

#1 A Case of Missing on Midthorpe
#2 A Case of Bloodshed in Benidorm

#1 The Anagramist
#2 The Frame

# Confusion in Cleethorpes
*A Sanford 3rd Age Club Mystery (#22)*

# Prologue

In a call for quiet, Joe Murray rapped his pen on the table sending ripples through the beer in his glass, the tonic water in Sheila Riley's, and the Campari in Brenda Jump's. "Let's have a bit of hush, people and hear what Mort has to say."

Mid-January, and it was a routine meeting of the Sanford 3rd Age Club, held in the top room of the Miners Arms. Its purpose was to decide the date and venue of the next STAC outing, and as always it was the subject of heated debate. The date had been settled but only after fierce argument. Some wanted Easter, others wanted before Easter, a few wanted after. Joe, Sheila and Brenda fell into the middle category by virtue of potential staff shortages at The Lazy Luncheonette over Easter and in the weeks immediately afterwards. At length, they got their way when the meeting decided upon a long weekend from Friday March twelfth to Monday the fifteenth (inclusive). Sanford Coach Services, the company they always used, would be engaged to ferry them from the Miners Arms to their destination and back again. All that remained was to decide upon that destination.

The decision had to be taken quickly. The nine or ten week lead time was vital if Joe, not only Chair of the club but also its chief negotiator, was to have any chance of getting them all into a hotel at a reasonable price, which was often at a good discount from the usual tariffs.

And as always, the suggestions were as varied as the members themselves.

Scarborough, Blackpool, Whitby were odds on joint favourites. Great Yarmouth and Weston-super-Mare were rank outsiders and soon dismissed as too far from Sanford, as were seaside locations in Devon, Cornwall, Essex and Northumberland. Alec and Julia Staines wanted Morecambe or the Lake District, precisely because their son lived in the area, Stewart Dalmer proposed Shrewsbury until someone pointed out that there was an antiques fair in the area and as an antiques dealer, Dalmer was making an effort to feather his Sanford nest rather than establishing a relaxing weekend for his fellow members. The meeting in general wanted somewhere more leisurely than Leeds, Manchester or Sheffield, and when George Robson suggested Benidorm, he was practically shouted down.

"It only takes three hours on the plane," he protested.

"And six hours hanging around airports," Les Tanner pointed out. "Hardly worth it for a couple of days."

"Then make it a week."

"We don't want a week," someone protested. "It's too near Easter."

"If I can just say summat…"

Mort Norris's words were drowned out as an argument spooled up between George and the last complainant, and when Mort tried to interrupt, he was shouted down. Eventually Joe intervened and asked for quiet. As the hubbub died down, he gave Mort an encouraging nod.

For as long as Joe could remember, Mort had owned a stall on Sanford market dealing in second-hand goods and general bric-a-brac. A small, generally unnoticeable man, now in his mid-fifties, he could never physically dominate any situation, but he was possessed of a glib tongue and a line of patter that ensured his moderate success in his chosen field. Rich he might not be, but he was comfortable within the boundaries of his modest ambitions.

"I wanna put an alternative to you." He nodded down at his disabled wife. "Alma is nigh on permanently stuck in her wheelchair these days, and a lot of these places have heaving great hills…"

"Blackpool doesn't," Owen Frickley objected.

"Neither does Morecambe," Alec Staines said.

Joe sighed. "Can we hear Mort out, please?"

"Thanks, Joe." Mort addressed the meeting again. "I know about Blackpool and Morecambe, but we've been there before. I wanna put forward a place we've never been, leastways not while I've been a member. Cleethorpes."

George Robson laughed. "There's a reason we've never been to Cleethorpes. It's the second most boring town in England after Withernsea."

Owen Frickley backed him up. "Last time I was there it was shut… and that was in August."

Mort turned on him. "I'm not thinking of you and tubby going out on the pull." He pointed an angry finger at George Robson as the 'tubby' in question. "I'm thinking of me and Alma, and other people who are getting on a bit and can't get around as like they used to."

"Call me tubby again and you won't be able to get about until—"

This time it was Brenda Jump who rattled for silence. "Knock it off, George, and he's right, Mort. You shouldn't be calling others. We're all friends, aren't we? Or we're supposed to be." She paused to let the simmering atmosphere cool a little. "Go on, Mort. What were you saying about Cleethorpes?"

"It's flat, it's quiet, and restful. And there's a big funfair for them as wants that kinda thing. And it ain't that far on the bus. Less than a coupla hours on the road. That's good for me and Alma."

Alongside Les Tanner, Sylvia Goodson spoke up. "I think Mort is right. I was only a child the last time I went to Cleethorpes, but I remember it as a pretty and pleasant little place, and if you want shopping or lively night life, it's only a few miles from Grimsby."

"And I have to confess, I've never been," Sheila said. "I'd be interested."

The discussion subsided and circulated and within a matter of minutes a vote was cast.

"Fifty one in favour, eight against, thirteen abstentions." Joe smiled upon the meeting. "That's it then. All names to Sheila, Brenda or me."

The meeting began to break up. People made for the bar, others for the toilets, and a queue formed at the dais where

Joe and his two friends began to list the names of interested parties. Their three names were at the top of the list, Tanner and Sylvia were beneath them, with the Staineses below them, and although Mort was slow to get there, Joe pencilled in him and his wife high up the list. Despite their complaints, George Robson and Owen Frickley were not slow to add their names. Twenty minutes later, Joe counted up the potential passengers, stood up and rapped his pen on the table once more.

"There you go, folks. Fifty odd people on board. I'll have a price for you by the weekend, and if you can let me have the moolah as soon as. I'll get onto the travel agent tomorrow, and after that, it's look out Cleethorpes, the Sanford 3rd Age Club are coming your way."

# Chapter One

It was Joe's experience that even during the busiest times of day, there were occasional lulls, and that applied to the breakfast queue of Sanford Brewery's draymen; a time when everyone was served and seated, some of the early arrival were gone, and for a few, brief minutes, there was no one waiting at the counter. Joe took advantage of that gap to assist Kayleigh, a temp brought in to cover Sheila's absence, as she cleared the tables.

It was a task Sheila would normally carry out as she delivered meals, but Joe had to make allowances for Kayleigh. A friend of his nephew's wife, the girl was a trier (although Joe had often been heard to comment that she was at her best when trying his patience) but she struggled to keep pace with the speedy turnover of meals, crockery and cutlery.

As with any departure from routine, seeing Joe come from behind the counter to help her, drew comments from the draymen, most of them ribald, some of them unrepeatable in polite company, and Joe gave as good as he received.

"So what's with you clearing the tables, Joe?" Barry Standish asked. "Been demoted, have you?"

"That's right. I decided my performance wasn't good enough, so I sent myself back to basics. I stopped short of giving myself a pay cut, though."

Barry chuckled. "Normally, you'd be having a quick and crafty smoke at the back door about now."

"Sheila's off this morning, isn't she? Hospital appointment."

Barry's humour faded. "Nothing serious, is it?"

"Routine." Joe stacked dirty, empty plates and beakers into a bread tray. "It's that business from the other Christmas. You know. After she got married and had all those tummy troubles."

"Courtesy, Mr—"

Joe interrupted. "Mister he who should never be named on pain of death by Sheila's handbag. But yeah, that's it. She has a check-up once a quarter just to make sure everything's as it should be."

"Good. He got what he deserved." Barry took out his tobacco and prepared a hand-rolled cigarette for consumption once out of the café. "Whisper is you're away this weekend… again."

"Tomorrow morning. Cleethorpes with the 3rd Age Club." Joe grinned.

Barry laughed. "Cleethorpes? You certainly know how to live, don't you?"

"You'll find out soon enough. It won't be long before you're joining us."

"On the promise of a weekend in Cleethorpes? Not likely. Besides, I couldn't keep pace with those tearaways. What are we gonna do for breakfast? Sid Snetterton's away, too, you know. His place is shut for a fortnight. Him and his missus are going to the Bahamas."

Joe sniffed. "Marvellous, innit? He runs a crummy snack bar and clears off to the Bahamas for a couple of weeks. I run the best caff in Sanford, and what do I get? Cleethorpes." He picked up the bread tray, ready for returning to the kitchen. "Anyway, you don't have to worry. Lee and Cheryl are on station for the weekend, and we'll be back on Tuesday morning."

Barry finished his tea, dropped the empty beaker into the bread tray, and signalled to his mate that it was time to get on with their day's work. "Funny time to go away, though, isn't it? The middle of March? I mean, it's only three weeks to Easter."

Joe's face fell again. "Ah, well, you see, we couldn't go over Easter because Lee and Cheryl are going to Ibiza or somewhere for a week, and when they get back Sheila and Brenda are having a week in Cyprus. There's only this bloody fool who gets no further than Cleethorpes." Joe pointed to his temple to indicate the 'bloody fool' in question.

Barry laughed again, more cynically this time. "Oh yeah? What about your ex-missus in Tenerife? According to George Robson, the last time you were there, you had your feet well under the table."

"And his underpants hanging on the washing line," Brenda called from the kitchen.

Joe refused to rise to the jibe. "Me and Alison were reminiscing on past glories, that's all."

"You're a dark horse, Joe," Barry said as he and his mate left. "They always say you little 'uns are the worst. We'll see you tomorrow… or when you get back from Cleethorpes."

Joe watched the two men, the last of the brewery crew, leave then carried the tray to the kitchen and dropped it on the worktop near the dishwasher.

Brenda was helping Lee, Joe's giant but genial nephew prepare the Ingleton Engineering order for delivery. "Reminiscing." She snorted disdain. "Trying to recapture your past glories, you mean. You couldn't resist her. All that skin she was showing?"

"What would you expect her to wear in the Canary Islands? Thermals and two jumpers?" Deliberately changing the subject, Joe went on, "She was a damn sight warmer than we'll be this weekend."

"Forecast is good, Uncle Joe," Lee said. "Flight pressure cone coming in from the Afores or somewhere."

"It's a high pressure zone," Joe corrected him. "And it's the Azores, not the afores. They're getting on for two thousand miles away so I don't think it'll get to Cleethorpes that fast."

Kayleigh arrived with another load of washing up, and the front door chimed to announce the arrival of four workmen from the retail park behind The Lazy Luncheonette, where they were carrying out repairs to the worn road surfaces. Leaving Kayleigh to stack the dishwasher Joe washed his hands and made his way to the counter to take their order.

He had stood behind that counter and its predecessor

(before that building burned down a few years earlier) for the better part of half a century, and there was nothing he did not know about the progress of an average day. From the arrival of the draymen between seven and half past, to locking the doors and setting the alarms at four in the afternoon, he could itemise every event, and the only things he could not forecast were Lee's occasional habit of dropping plates and Kayleigh's inability to distinguish between full cream, semi-skimmed, and skimmed milk. The latter was not a major issue, since she worked to cover absences and then only occasionally. Such was his ingrained knowledge that he could tell when the middle-aged, overweight woman from the solicitor's office next door would choose cappuccino and when she would opt for still water, a factor, he reasoned, of her bathroom scales and whether she had gained or lost weight.

He was not alone. Sheila, Brenda, and Lee had all worked with him for almost a decade, and Lee's wife, Cheryl, had come on-board part-time once their son, Danny, started school. She would arrive at half past nine, and leave again at half past two. They, too, knew the ropes, were able to handle anything and everything the day's customers threw at them.

And yet there was nothing magic about it. It was simply experience. As a young teenager, he had helped his father behind the counter before and after school, and at the age of sixteen, he walked out of school and straight into full-time work at Alf's Café, as it was known then, with one day per week at Sanford Technical College. Even then, he would be in the café before leaving for college.

It all made for a successful business, and if Joe was not quite as wealthy as some people imagined, he had a comfortable life. Lonely now and then, true, but thanks to the 3rd Age Club, which he, Sheila, and Brenda had founded, he had plenty of friends.

As the proprietor – senior partner since granting his three senior employees shares in the cafe – he also had the luxury of taking time off whenever he felt he needed it, and the 3rd Age Club's occasional weekend outings allowed him to wallow in that freedom. It had to be arranged around other matters, such as Lee and Cheryl's upcoming holiday, and that of Sheila and Brenda, but he needed no one's permission to take a couple of days off for a long weekend.

Despite his muted complaints to Barry, an example of his legendary grumpiness, he was actively looking forward to the weekend. It had been a difficult winter. Bitterly cold around New Year and for most of January, not much of an improvement during February, and March had come in with all the venom of a black widow spider. The only respite, and that had been brief, was the annual Sanford 3rd Age Club dinner and dance on Valentine's night, but Joe had been unable to secure a date, and ended up accompanying Brenda, a great friend, a valuable colleague, but one who frequently reminded him of that same black widow spider feeling the peckish urge of the mating season.

Cleethorpes would make a welcome change. It might not be the liveliest resort in Great Britain but it was less than seventy miles from Sanford. Their bus was scheduled to leave the Miners Arms at ten on Friday morning, and it was practically certain that Keith Lowry, their regular driver, would have them in their hotel by noon. From there, it would be a weekend of relaxation and – if Joe knew Sheila and Brenda – retail therapy. Four days without the need to crawl out of bed at five in the morning, four days without having to worry about the bookkeeping, orders from the cash-and-carry, delivery drivers turning up at all hours, and the constant queue of Sanford's ever hungry inhabitants, four days without the inevitable minor burns from hot appliances, four days of taking a shower for reasons other than to get the stink of the kitchen out of his nostrils… four days of freedom.

Life, he told himself as the first customers from the offices above and around them arrived, could be much worse.

\*\*\*

As long as it was not occupied by paying customers, table five, immediately in front of and to the left of the service counter, was designated as the staff 'rest area', where they took their morning breaks, and they did so on a rota basis. Lee and Joe were first to arrive every morning and while Lee took his break at half past nine, after the rush was over, Joe pressed on until half past ten, which allowed him to take half an hour off in the company of Sheila and Brenda. Kayleigh took her break with Lee, but then, she would be on her way home after the lunchtime rush was over, and Lee would be gone by half past two. As with every other aspect of life at The Lazy Luncheonette, the system worked.

By the time Joe knocked off and Brenda returned from delivering the Ingleton Engineering order, Sheila was also back and Cheryl was on hand to assist in the kitchen and man the counter. While Joe concentrated on the cryptic crossword in the Daily Express, Sheila gave Brenda a blow by blow account of her visit to the hospital, which according to Joe, listening with half an ear, could be summarised with the words, 'there's nothing wrong with me'.

He refrained from saying so. He and the two women had been the very best of friends for half a century. Time and experience had taught him when to mind his own business, when to keep his mouth shut.

Kayleigh appeared alongside him. "Could I have a word, Mr Murray?"

He put down his pen and smiled up. "Only if you promise to call me Joe."

She sat at table six across the aisle from him. "I don't like. My mum says I should respect old people."

Joe frowned at the word 'old'. "Your mum's right, but we work as a team here. Strictly first names. Now what's up?"

"I just wondered whether there was any chance of something more, er, permanent. I don't mean full-time, but something more regular."

Despite his often undeserved reputation, Joe was never unkind, and it was part of his nature to feel compassion for a young woman like this, struggling to find employment.

On the other hand, she was not the brightest spark in The Lazy Luncheonette's box of matches. As he considered her request, a mental image of profit and loss accounts materialised in his head, and he searched for an excuse. "It's not something I can decide on, Kayleigh. I don't own the business outright. Not anymore. Sheila, Brenda and Lee are all partners, and I have to take their opinions on board. But I'll tell you what I'll do. We're going away for the weekend, so you'll be working tomorrow, Saturday, and Monday. I'll speak to Sheila, Brenda, and Lee this afternoon, and I'll let you know when we get back. Are you getting desperate?"

Kayleigh's pretty face twisted into a mask of agonised doubt. "Not desperate. Not really. But I could do with something. Right now, I'm allowed to work sixteen hours a week without it affecting my benefits, but working here is casual. Cash in hand, and I can't tell them about it. If I have something regularer, I could tell them and they'd be okay. It'd be much better if I could tell them that I'm, sort of, permanent. You see what I mean?"

Still struggling with the word 'regularer', Joe reached across the aisle and patted her hand. "No promises but leave it with me, and I'll see what we can do."

# Chapter Two

Rose Louden checked her appearance in the three-quarter length, wardrobe mirror and happy that it would not yield any secrets, sat in the small armchair beneath the window, and concentrated on Paul Caswell, trombonist with the Shoreline Swingsters, the band which she fronted as chief vocalist. "So tell me, what was Cam hassling you about… as if I don't already know."

"The usual." Caswell gave her his favourite, most charming smile, the one which had first tempted her so many years ago.

If she was an attractive and shapely forty-four-year-old strawberry blonde, he was her male counterpart. A couple of years younger than her, good-looking, muscular, one of life's natural bachelors and charmers. A head of jet black hair, midnight eyes and that easy smile, so seductive, so welcoming, all coupled to an insouciance which won him many friends and lovers, and so irritated his male competitors. And the fact that she was married to the bandleader had never dissuaded him from plying his charms on her.

Neither did it prevent her from falling under their spell. Her husband was almost ten years older than her, and it had to be said that if fifteen years of marriage to Tommy had taught her anything, it was her place in the grand scheme of Tommy's hierarchy. His main interests, in order of importance were, himself, the band, the clarinet, which he played, and music in general. She came never better than fifth, and at times she was lower down the scale than that. She loved the band, loved being in the spotlight, delivering her raucous voice to appreciative audiences, revelling in their applause. But coming a poor fifth on her husband's order of priorities was simply not good enough.

And so she compensated.

"That's a new word for it," Caswell would often joke after they passed an afternoon together.

Did Tommy know? If not, it said much about his perception of the world around him.

Caswell, a better than average trombonist, was also the band's accountant, and Rose controlled the money, which meant that, no matter where they were appearing, they had regular meetings, but even Tommy, a man obsessed with Glenn Miller, the Dorsey Brothers, Ella Fitzgerald, et al, should be asking himself just how many meetings it should take to decide who would be paid how much and how often.

In her more reflective moments, she would often persuade herself that Tommy did know and had decided that as long as she and Caswell were discreet and their antics did not interfere with the band, they could carry on. Such thoughts often brought out the rebellious anger in her. She had married a mouse. He had married her purely to tie her to the Shoreline Swingsters. He was secretly gay. A range of conclusions, not one of which had any supportive evidence, but which manifested within her to the point where she had to be careful not to bring matters to a head.

Caswell was more open with her. She had lost count of the times he had suggested they cut away from the band and branch out on their own. "I'm not just a slidy Sam, you know. I can go some on keyboards and you are one of the best jazz singers on the circuit. We'd be better off."

She would not do it. Grateful as she was for his compliments, a voice as powerful as hers and the repertoire in which she specialised needed serious backing, not just a piano.

Through the single window of his room at the Sunbeam Guest House, the main shopping street of Cleethorpes laboured under a sunny but cold Friday in March. At odds with the sunshine, shoppers were few and far between, and Rose was bored. She longed for the official start of the season (Easter as near as she could judge) still three weeks away, and the crowds which would flock to the bar of the

Queen Elizabeth Hotel where the Shoreline Swingsters were booked for a dozen performances a week until September. With the bar and ballroom open to non-residents as well as paying guests, she anticipated a packed house every afternoon and evening.

But for the last month it had been rehearse, rehearse, and rehearse, playing to an empty room while Tommy got his power kick from screaming at them for the occasional flat note and more frequent lack of verve.

The rustle of Caswell pulling on his shirt, covering that muscle-packed chest, brought her attention back into the room. "So go on. What did Cam have to say to you?"

"What he always says. He wants more money." Caswell laughed. "I think he's having trouble with his bookie again."

It was a familiar tale. Trumpet player, Campbell Arnholt was good – he had to be or he would not be with the Shoreline Swingsters – but like Tommy Louden, he could be temperamental and in the three years since he joined the band, he had dogged them with his financial grumbles. Child support for the offspring of a broken marriage, and an uncontrollable gambling habit left him broke most of the time, and he was never shy to grouse on the pay rates.

"Stupid question, but can we afford to pay him more?" Rose watched Caswell pull on his leather bomber jacket.

"No." Caswell zipped up the jacket and reached for his crash helmet. "Not unless you cut out accountancy fees." He laughed again. "But I'm not going to do the books for nothing, and frankly, if I left it to you and Tommy, the whole band would be paying more in taxes." He put the helmet in place and left the visor up. "They'd each need an accountant, and I'd probably end up making even more. Cam will just have to whistle for it… or blow his horn somewhere else." He passed Rose her leathers and helmet. "We'd better get a move on. There's a coach party due in this afternoon, and your old man will expect us on top form tonight."

\*\*\*

When it came to the weather, Lee proved the more accurate forecaster. Friday morning greeted Sanford with a blaze of sunshine but it was tempered by a chilly wind when Joe climbed into a taxi outside his house for the ten-minute journey to the Miners Arms.

True to his word, he had a brief chat with Lee the previous afternoon regarding Kayleigh's request, and learned, not much to his surprise, that his nephew was in favour.

"She's a bit of a numpty sometimes, Uncle Joe. Look at the time when she put yoghurt instead of milk in the bar vista machine."

Lee had graduated from naming the 'barista' as 'bar vista' after originally calling it 'bar mitzvah', and it compelled Joe to wonder how anyone capable of such confusion would have the sheer neck to describe Kayleigh as a 'numpty' but then, Lee – like his uncle – had always been plain spoken, even if it was often to the puzzlement of others.

"But she's good-hearted and a good worker," Lee concluded.

A brace of unofficial endorsements which placed Kayleigh alongside the rest of The Lazy Luncheonette's crew, Joe thought, and promised his nephew he would consult with Sheila and Brenda before making a decision.

A busier than expected Thursday afternoon, the women's eagerness to be away as soon as possible in order to pack for Cleethorpes, and Joe's desire to ensure Lee and Cheryl were well briefed for the weekend, denied him the opportunity, and he resolved to speak to them on the journey to North East Lincolnshire.

Before he could do that, however, there were other duties to be performed, and the first one was to ensure the members who had paid for the weekend were all present and correct.

When he climbed out of his taxi at the Miners Arms, he relieved Sheila of the passenger list, allowing her to board the bus out of the cold, while Joe took over the name check.

Aside from a brief period after the death of Denise Latham, when Les Tanner took over, Joe had been Chair of the Sanford 3rd Age Club ever since its inception five years previously.

Sheila acted as secretary and Brenda the Treasurer. None of the roles was particularly onerous, but it was the responsibility of the managerial triumvirate to ensure that those members who had paid for outings and excursions were on the bus before it departed, and more importantly, were there for the return journey. It was also a part of their duty to ensure that tickets for any shows or events were issued to the members, but there was nothing scheduled for the forthcoming weekend in Cleethorpes. Once checked into the hotel, another task Joe and the two women often had to supervise, the members were free to come and go as they pleased.

"So are we all geared up for a mind blowing rave on Grimsby fish dock?" George Robson commented as he and his closest friend, Owen Frickley, boarded the coach and made for the rear seat.

Joe ticked their names on the passenger list, and responded, "Whatever turns you on, George."

Keith Lowry, one of Sanford Coach Services senior drivers, was loading the members' bags into the underslung luggage rack, and paused after throwing Owen Frickley's sports bag in above George Robson's small case. "What I can never understand is why you and your crumblies choose to go to nowhere in the middle of winter."

Keith was regularly assigned to the 3rd Age Club's excursions and holidays, and despite his grumbling – almost a match for Joe, some people said – he got on well with most of the members.

"It's not winter, it's spring," Joe argued as he checked off Norman and Irene Pyecock, two of the club's oldest members.

Keith fingered the sleeve of Joe's quilted topcoat. "Then why are you wearing your eiderdown, wrapped up like an Eskimo?"

"I believe they're known as Inuits," Sheila said as she climbed off the coach to help Irene board.

"All right, why is he still wearing his Inuit and wrapped up like an Eskimo?"

Joe sniffed disdainfully. "I have it on the best authority

that the weekend will be sunny and warm."

"Whose authority?" Keith demanded.

"Our Lee."

"That's it, then. If your Lee says it's gonna be warm and sunny, I should have brought my snowshoes."

"Just shut up moaning and tell me where we'll be stopping for a brew."

Keith was aghast. "Stopping? It's less than seventy miles, Joe. We'll be all the way there in less than two hours."

Joe would not hear it. "You know what this lot are like. And if you don't know what they're like, you should know what their bladders are like. They'll be lucky to get to Doncaster without needing the lavatory."

"The old man's expecting me back early afternoon, in time for the school run."

"You're not staying with us?"

"If I'm supposed to know your lot better, then you should know what he's like, Joe. You've nothing planned for the weekend, so I have to be back. Schools today, a football special tomorrow, and a Merseyside car boot sale on Sunday before I come back to Cleethorpes to pick you up on Monday afternoon."

"Well, he's a cheeky sod. The amount of money we pay him—"

Keith cut Joe off. "According to him, he runs your trips at a loss."

"And according to me The Lazy Luncheonette is the gourmet capital of Europe, but that doesn't make it true. All I'm saying is, you've done enough of our weekends to know that this lot will need the lavatory, a cuppa and a smoke before you get to Scunthorpe."

The driver gave up the unwinnable argument. "Doncaster services. Just before we join the M180. It's only about half an hour from here, and after that it's straight through to Cleethorpes. About an hour. Make sure they all know."

Content that he had won the argument, Joe returned to his task in hand, and checked in Alec and Julia Staines, and Mort and Alma Norris. While Keith carefully folded and stashed

Alma's small power-wheelchair into the luggage compartment, Sheila climbed off the bus again and with Julia's assistance, helped Alma board.

Mort followed the operation with some concern.

"She'll be all right, Mort," Joe assured him.

"I don't like to see her like this, Joe."

There was no safe answer to that, so Joe encouraged him and Alec to get on the bus, and checked his list again. "Only Mavis Barker and Cyril Peck to come and we can get going."

"You get on and chat your grumbly crumblies up, Joe," Keith suggested. "I'll wait for those two."

"Roger, dodger."

Joe was relieved to be out of the wind, and as he boarded the coach, he removed his topcoat, and stored it on the overhead rack above Sheila and Brenda. Reaching to the window pillar just ahead of their seat, he unclipped the PA mike, tapped the head to ensure it was working, and then began to speak.

"Well, morning, everybody. We're only waiting for Mavis and Cyril, and we'll be on our way. Keith reckoned no more than an hour and a half to Cleethorpes, but I persuaded him to stop at Doncaster Services to break the journey. After that, it'll be straight through to Cleethorpes, so ye of the weak bladders, tie a knot in it or buy some incontinence knickers, and all you smokers, stoke up your nicotine levels while we're stopped."

"You're the biggest smoker on the bus, Joe," George Robson called from the rear seat.

"I lead from the front, George, so I'll be filling up at Doncaster."

Closer to Joe, Les Tanner, head of the payroll department at Sanford Town Hall and a former captain in the Territorial Army Reserve, snorted. "You're not tall enough to lead anyone, Murray."

Brenda half turned in her seat. "Yes he is. He's highly skilled at leading us into temptation."

Joe frowned. "I wouldn't mind them talking about me if they did it behind my back."

Brenda grinned at him. "You mean like me, Joe?"

As a ragged laugh ran through the fifty or so passengers, Joe turned to find Mavis Barker standing behind him, waiting to pass, and beyond her was Cyril Peck. Joe shuffled sideways into the vacant seats across the aisle from Sheila and Brenda, and while Mavis and Cyril took their seats, Keith settled behind the wheel, started the engine and closed the automatic door.

"Park your carcass, Joe, we're up and running."

With a half-hearted cheer from the passengers, Keith pulled off the pub car park, turning right for the motorway. Joe stood, put the microphone back, settled into the seat opposite across from his two closest friends, and took out his phone.

"Texting, Joe?" Brenda asked.

"Reading." He opened the e-reader app. "Your idea, Brenda. You're always listening to music on your phone, and you know how I like to read when we're on the bus, so I thought it's better than carrying paperbacks with me."

"I also know how you nod off to sleep on the bus and drop the paperback on the floor. Don't drop your phone or you'll need a new one."

Joe ignored the remark, and opened his copy of Fleming's Moonraker.

"Oh, look. Lee's sweeping up broken plates again."

Brenda's comment caused Joe to abandon his reading, and look up sharply, turning his head to gaze on The Lazy Luncheonette as the bus passed, only to learn that Brenda was teasing him. With a scowl, he returned to the machinations of Bond and Galatea Brand.

He had read the book any number of times since becoming hooked on the Bond novels in his late teens, but as the only novel in the series set exclusively in England (albeit London and Kent) it seemed appropriate in the light of the prospective weekend in Lincolnshire. Not that he anticipated coming across many foreign spies or rogue nuclear missiles in Cleethorpes, but when travelling with some of the more eccentric members of the 3rd Age Club, there would inevitably be some excitement.

Beyond the M62's junction with the A1, the view ahead opened up to a spectacular vista taking in the flat plain of East Yorkshire, North and South Humberside and North Lincolnshire, the landscape dominated by the giant cooling towers of Eggborough and Drax power stations, and Joe recalled that years before, there had been a third; Thorpe Marsh, to the north of Doncaster. And somewhere amongst those green, agricultural bands, along with the inland docks of Goole, slightly to the south were the slag heaps of Doncaster's main collieries. Landscaped and grassed over these days, they were the remains of an all but defunct industry which had helped power the Industrial Revolution.

Less than fifteen miles east of the A1, Keith pulled off to join the M18, turning south towards Doncaster, and a little over a quarter of an hour later, where it met the M180, instead of turning right for the Lincolnshire coast, he turned right into Doncaster Services. Joe checked his watch. It was less than forty minutes since they left the Miners Arms.

Shunting his vehicle into one of the designated coach parks, Keith switched on his PA system.

"All right, crumblies. You've got three quarters of an hour. If you're not back on the bus by then, I'll leave without you."

"Idle threats," Joe muttered as she climbed off the coach.

He and the two women were always first to alight, and they waited by the door to assist the more elderly, less agile members, but with time short, Joe elected to stay while Sheila assisted Alma Norris, and Brenda went ahead into the cafeteria to arrange coffee and snacks.

Ten minutes later, with everyone off the bus, making their way into the building, Joe and Sheila joined Brenda at a window table.

"I hope Lee, Cheryl and Kayleigh are managing all right," Sheila said. "Three people is a bit thin for a Friday morning."

"That friend of theirs, Pauline, is coming in too, isn't she, Joe?"

Joe nodded in answer to Brenda's question. "They'll cope. And talking of Kayleigh, she's asked me if we can take her on permanently. I meant to mention it before, but I forgot. I asked Lee yesterday afternoon and he's in favour, but let's face it, he's not the brightest when it comes to making decisions."

Sheila helped herself to an iced fancy. "You're the boss, Joe, so it's your decision."

Taking out his tobacco tin and rolling a cigarette, he disagreed. "You're partners remember, so you have as much say as me. Paying her a wage permanently, will reduce the profits and your share."

"She's a good kid," Brenda declared. "She's never let you down yet."

Joe clucked impatiently. "You've obviously forgotten last Christmas when she asked a customer if she'd like gravy with her mince pie."

Sheila tutted and Brenda laughed. "The woman did see the funny side of it," Brenda said.

Sheila supported her friend's observation. "And Kayleigh did ask the woman rather than just pouring gravy over it."

"She might be willing, but she's as brainless as Lee. Can we afford more than one dipstick?"

Sheila became more serious. "She'll need training, and while we're training her, she'll need watching carefully, but aside from that, how much will she cost us in terms of personal income? A few hundred pounds a quarter between the four of us. I'm sure we can stand it, and you have to feel sorry for her. It must be hell trying to find work in a town like Sanford when you have no qualifications."

"And talking of qualifications," Brenda said, "she'll have to take a Food Hygiene Certificate course. You've managed to get away with it so far, Joe, but if she's coming on permanently, she'll have to go for it. I think it's a couple of days, isn't it?"

Joe nodded. "And we'll have to pay for it. Well, The Lazy Luncheonette will have to pay for it."

"Why not give her a chance, Joe? She is hard-working."

"Not to mention hard work. I'll give it a coat of thinking about, and I promised her an answer by Tuesday when we're back."

# Chapter Three

Fifty miles ahead of them, in the reception lobby of the Queen Elizabeth Hotel, the manager, Armand Turgot (he insisted it was pronounced tur-go and not tur-got) was having similar problems with an assistant housekeeper to those Joe anticipated with Kayleigh. It was not that Vicky Ordish was unwilling to work, but she struggled to understand certain procedures.

"When one hears those kinds of noises coming from a room, it is a signal for housekeepers to pass by the door. Not knock, walk in, and say 'I won't be ten minutes, luvs'."

A furious blush came to Vicky's cheeks. "But they hadn't put the 'do not disturb' sign up, Mr Turgot. How was I supposed to know?"

"It's called discretion, Miss Ordish. Putting out the DND notice is not enshrined in English law. You heard unidentifiable noises coming from the room, you should not have entered. Mr Bickerstaffe was most annoyed when he checked out."

"They were only dancing, Mr Turgot. It's not like they were—"

"Irrelevant. They were professional dancers rehearsing their routine for a ballroom competition to be held in Lincoln next week. They are entitled to their privacy. Concentration is vital to such professionals, and as a result of your barging in on them, they lost it. I shall refrain from making a note on your personnel file, but if we get any more such instances, I'll have no alternative but to refer you for further training. Do you understand?"

"Yes, Mr Turgot."

"Very well. Get on with your work."

While she went about her duties, Turgot returned to the reception counter, and opened up the bookings account on the computer.

He was expecting the imminent arrival of the Sanford 3rd Age Club. A large booking, profitable too, notwithstanding the discount the negotiator, a certain Joseph Murray, had secured with head office. They were, so he was assured, old and valued customers, and a phone call to Yvonne Vallance, manager of the Palmer Hotel near York, where he had worked for some time during his younger years, confirmed that while the group was comprised of seniors, they were anything but old and fuddy-duddy.

Yvonne spoke about them in glowing terms, particularly Murray, who, for reasons Turgot could not quite understand, was partly responsible for her marriage to her assistant (at the time), Geoffrey Vallance.

Turgot thanked her for the information, but in keeping with the hierarchical structures lodged in his head, considered her marriage to a subordinate to be incompatible with her managerial status, and he marked Yvonne down several points.

Aged forty-four, born in Gateshead, the son of a hotel porter, he had never considered any other career than the leisure sector, and before he left school, he narrowed his choices down to the hotel industry. His education ended with a few, largely meaningless, GCSEs, and from the moment he signed on with his present employer, starting as a humble booking clerk, he had only one target in sight; the general manager of a five-star establishment.

And he worked assiduously towards his goal, inculcating a finely tuned, classless accent, delivering (in his opinion) perfect English with every word, and slowly, surely, he rose through the ranks, until now he was on one of the lower rungs of the ladder to his ultimate target. The Queen Elizabeth Hotel, situated on the seafront in Cleethorpes, barely scraped three stars, but he was not disheartened. He had over twenty years to go until the earliest date of his retirement. Ample time to achieve his ambition, namely overall control of a five-star hotel. Catering for a large group such as the Sanford 3rd Age Club, might just be a leg up to the next step.

Naturally, it meant coming down hard on his staff, in the same way that the managers had come down hard on him when he was younger. From the housekeepers and assistant housekeepers, whom he refused to refer to as 'chambermaids', to the maître d' of the dining room, he demanded first-class service and absolute obedience.

And if there were any blots on the horizon, any potential barriers to what he saw as his inexorable rise to power, a brace of examples came through the revolving doors as Vicky left him: Rose Louden and Paul Caswell, respectively lead vocalist and trombonist with the Shoreline Swingsters, the Queen Elizabeth's resident band for the forthcoming season.

About the same age as Turgot, tall, muscular, shifty-eyed, Caswell was the kind of man who, in the 1930s, would have been described as a lounge lizard. He had a lackadaisical attitude about him, one Turgot did not care for, but the band had a contract with the hotel, and Turgot had almost no control over him or his nine colleagues.

Rose Louden was a different, but paradoxically a similar proposition. Five feet four inches tall, a head of blonde-ish hair and a shapely figure, and an attitude which firmly entrenched her as the wife of the bandleader. Turgot had heard her singing during the month that the band had spent rehearsing in the ballroom, and in his selective opinion, she was better suited to pitching from a market stall. He kept to himself the thought of what she should be selling, but it centred around her stage attire – body-hugging gowns with deep cleavages.

Coming into the hotel via the front entrance was, however, a clear breach of the rules he spelled out on first meeting the band. To begin with, their attire was unsuitable. The whole band were fine on stage. The men clad in smart blazers and black ties, the women in various, low-cut, ankle-length, sometimes skin-tight dresses, complete with the necessary glitter. But as they walked in through reception, a route neither of them was authorised to take, Caswell was wearing a pair of scruffy jeans and a leather, bomber jacket, zipped up to keep out the March chill. A pair of stout boots and a motorcyclist's crash helmet swinging from one hand finalised the appearance of a Hell's Angel, totally unbecoming with a hotel of the Queen Elizabeth's standing, even if that status reigned largely in Turgot's imagination.

Rose Louden was similarly clad in a set of motorcycle leathers, and she, too, carried her crash helmet.

"How many times do I have to tell you, Mrs Louden, Mr Caswell, your route into the hotel is the tradesmen's entrance around the side of the building?"

"The bin wagon's there. We couldn't get in," Rose said.

"Besides, what are you worrying about?" Caswell waved around the empty reception area. "It's not like you've got a cast of thousands hanging around, is it?"

"We expect a large party arriving any time."

Caswell smacked his lips. "Youngsters? Available wives having a weekend away from their husbands?"

"Delectable young men slavering for it?" Rose laughed.

Turgot ignored their teasing. "They're an upmarket group of senior citizens, and I expect you and your colleagues to behave with a certain amount of decorum."

Caswell, about to follow Rose to the ballroom, grinned. "Decorum? Isn't that what you do to apples before you put them in a pie?" Laughing uproariously to himself, he went on his way.

Behind him, Turgot's lips curled in disdain. "If I had my way…"

But the Shoreline Swingsters had a cast iron contract, and no matter how much he would like to see the back of them, especially Caswell, Turgot could do nothing.

\*\*\*

It was on the tail end of the argument that Joe and Brenda walked in.

The Queen Elizabeth Hotel stood in proud isolation on

Alexandra Road, opposite Pier Gardens. A four-storey, redbrick edifice, its ground floor windows boasting sandstone bays, and although it claimed to be a seafront establishment, it was set back from the real seafront by a hundred yards, a consequence of the road splitting near the hotel, and the promenade (with ample parking) running parallel to Alexandra Road, closer to the beach and at a lower level. As a consequence, when the Sanford 3rd Age Club members disembarked, the only glimpse they had of the sea was through gaps in the trees lining the gardens.

Taking the passenger list from Sheila, as Joe and Brenda prepared to enter reception, he looked up. "The rooms at the front should get a smashing view of Belgium from their windows."

"Southern Denmark where it borders the Netherlands and Germany, Joe," Sheila corrected him as she made ready to help the older members from the coach. "Belgium is much further south. Straight across the sea from Ramsgate, if memory serves."

Joe led the way in. "It's what I love about the 3rd Age Club. Not only fun, but educational. I mean, Brenda, could you have made it through the weekend without that geography lesson from Sheila?"

"You know what she's like, Joe. She likes things right and she was a school secretary for most of her working life."

Ahead of them Rose and Caswell walked away from reception, and Turgot glowered thunder after them.

"Doesn't look too promising," Brenda commented. "Ooh, look. The entertainment."

Joe followed her pointing finger to a free-standing easel affair, supporting a large, sky-blue board decked with photographs of the Shoreline Swingsters. In the centre was a large, landscape-oriented image of the whole band, surrounded by individual photographs of the different members, each of them named.

Joe, who had never cared for swing music, screwed up his face. "Swingsters? Why not Swingers?" He pointed out the headline across the top of the board: *'all your favourites from the swing era'*. "I mean they play big band stuff from the thirties and forties, don't they, and that's swing music, so why not…" he trailed off as Brenda cackled. "What? What have I said?"

Brenda brought her mirth under control. "Seriously, Joe, what century are you living in? Swingers has a completely different meaning these days. It's like…" She racked her mind. "It's like you and me and Les Tanner and Sylvia getting together and swapping—"

Realisation clicked in Joe's head and he cut her off. "Don't go there. Please." He shuddered. "There's only so much my brain can take."

Chuckling between themselves, they approached reception under the disdainful glower of Armand Turgot.

"Afternoon, sport," Joe greeted.

"Good afternoon, sir." Turgot invested the word 'sir' with sufficient contempt to make his feelings clear. "How may I help you?"

"We wanna check in."

"Well, I'm sorry, but we're full." Turgot's voice made it clear that sorrow was the last emotion he felt.

"Just a minute, hang about, Mr Turgot—"

Joe pronounced the final letter of Turgot's name and it compelled the manager to interrupt. "It's Turgot… tur-go."

"Whatever you wanna call yourself. How can you be full? We have reservations."

The announcement did nothing to assuage Turgot's irritation. "And you are?"

Joe was beginning to tire of the lordly attitude. "Yes. I am. I'm thinking Kant. Cogs in the toe, here goes some."

"I think you will find it's Descartes and it's *cogito ergo sum*."

"Good. Now that we've finished with Sheila's geography, Brenda's explanation of your band's name, and your philosophy debate, will you please check us in?"

"Your name?"

"Joe Murray. This is Brenda Jump. We're part responsible for the Sanford 3rd Age Club. We've got fifty tired old gits on the bus, and some of them will be busting for the lavatory."

"Ah, yes. I was talking to Yvonne Vallance at the Palmer Hotel about you. I must say, I expected someone rather more socially adroit."

"We've had one like him before," Joe said to Brenda. "That old bat in Windermere. What was her name?"

"Atkinson." Brenda smiled at Turgot. "She didn't like Joe's shorts."

"I sympathise. And I haven't seen him in shorts. Now, Mr Murray, we have twenty eight rooms reserved for you and your party, but everyone must complete a registration card before I will issue keys."

"And your lobby's gonna be crowded if you make 'em queue up," Joe pointed out. "At other hotels, including the Palmer, the management give us the cards and we hand 'em out, and as they fill 'em in, the members can come to you for the keys."

Turgot began to count out the registration cards.

"Is the bar open?" Brenda asked.

"Yes, madam."

"They'll probably congregate in there, have a couple of snorts while they're filling in the cards."

It was clear that Turgot was not the happiest of men, and Joe elected to wind him up further. "How was Yvonne? Good looking lass, you know. Crikey, if I were twenty years younger, Geoff Vallance wouldn't have stood a chance."

"That, sir, sums up my opinion of her." Turgot handed over the cards. "I've given you thirty registration cards, against the dangers of elderly, shaking hands making a mess of the job. I assume all your people can write?"

"Check out the wall of the gents tomorrow."

Joe turned to walk away, but Brenda was not through. "You are aware, Mr Turgot, that some of our members have difficulty with stairs, and one of our lady members is wheelchair bound?"

"We do have elevators, madam, and yes, your original booking made us aware of the lady in question, and that some members of your party are semi-ambulatory. We accommodate them on the first floor."

"Thank you. By the way, they're lifts, not elevators. We're not American… or French." Brenda turned and hurried after Joe.

"Snooty git," Joe declared, making no effort to keep his voice down. "I meanersay, semi-ambulatory? Did someone buy him a dictionary for Christmas?"

"I don't know and I don't care, Joe. I'm not gonna let him spoil our stay here." She huddled close to him. "But I'm willing to let you make my weekend."

Joe shrugged her off with a grin. "Can't do it. I'm in love with Yvonne Vallance."

## Chapter Four

"What's that sticking up out of the water?" Sheila pointed to a small, circular building clearly visible a couple of miles down the beach and sitting just offshore in the shallow waters.

"World War One gun fort," Joe said. "There are two of them. Haile Sand and Bull Sand. Can't remember which is which, but the one stands just offshore here, and the other is off Spurn Point, actually inside the Humber Estuary."

"Bull Sand is a mile and a half off Spurn Point. The one you're looking at is Haile Sand." When they turned to gaze in amazement at Brenda's unexpected knowledge of the area, she had a smug grin across her face, and held up her smartphone. "Internet on the go."

"Smartarse."

"Granted."

Turgot's snooty attitude was not reflected in his excellent administrative abilities. He had worked quickly and accurately at the hotel's computer, while Vicky Ordish handed out keys and directions, and all fifty Sanford 3rd-agers were registered and in their rooms before two o'clock. As Turgot promised, the more elderly members were allocated rooms on the lower floors, and there were porters to assist with their minimal luggage.

The process was not without incident. As Joe stood by, collecting his key, a tall, beefy individual approached reception. By the look of the manner in which his arms were pushed out from his upper torso, he was muscular, but not particularly fit, as indicated by his distended abdomen. Under a shock of curly, jet black hair, his eyes were narrowed to pinpoints of irritation, and when he spoke, his mouth, mostly hidden behind a dark beard and bushy moustache, barely moved.

He spoke directly to Turgot. "Have you seen that git, Caswell?"

True to himself, Turgot looked down his nose, a remarkable feat considering that the newcomer was several inches taller than him. "I have repeatedly told you, Mr Arnholt, not to use this entrance. As you can see, I'm busy with check-ins. I told your colleague, Mr Caswell, the same earlier on. And I think you'll find him in the ballroom. In future, kindly use the tradesmen's entrance, along with the other staff."

Arnholt let out a snort, turned and pushed his way past Joe, who glowered after him before switching his attention to Turgot. "You don't get on too well with your entertainment crew, do you? That's the second argument you've had with them since we arrived."

"They find it difficult to adhere to rules and regulations, Mr Murray."

"Just wait while our lot start playing musical beds."

The check-in process complete, Joe and the women were posted to rooms on the third, uppermost floor (the fourth floor was given over to staff accommodation). Sheila and Brenda were granted a sea view, while Joe's single room overlooked the Queen Elizabeth's rear yard with its refuse bins and empty beer barrels and crates.

"Typical. I always get the crap view," he grumbled to himself while he unpacked his bags.

At three o'clock, compact camera in his pocket, he called for his two friends, and rather than join their fellow members in the hotel bar, they made their way out, through Pier Gardens, where local authority workers were attending the lawns and flowerbeds, and cleaning up the statues, presumably preparing for the start of the summer season, and onto the promenade, where they turned towards the short pier, a quarter of a mile to their left, and as they ambled along, Sheila posed her question on the gun fort.

Joe freely admitted that the only reason he knew anything about the forts was because he overheard Les Tanner boring the socks off Sylvia Goodson on the bus, and like Brenda, he used his smartphone to check the accuracy of Tanner's tale.

"Les got most of it right, but what he didn't say was that Haile Sand is for sale, and both of them are listed buildings, so if you fancy buying one of them, Sheila, you won't be able to make many alterations."

"Particularly to the fifteen-inch guns on the battlements," Brenda said.

The light-hearted quip generated fresh chuckles between the three.

The spread of the Humber Estuary lay before them, and the tide was so far out that it was difficult to see where Cleethorpes Beach ended and the official sea began. Further out, a large, low-slung cargo boat, possibly a tanker, plodded its way along the estuary making for the docks at Hull, Immingham or Goole, and beyond it, a passenger ferry sailed in the opposite direction.

"Rotterdam? Zeebrugge?" Joe speculated.

"It has to be one of those two," Sheila replied. "I don't think they sail to Ostend from here."

Brenda slipped into nostalgia again. "We did Rotterdam, didn't we? When we went to Amsterdam that time."

"Yes. And Joe was accused of murder on the way back."

"Well, that's what I'm here for, isn't it? If something goes wrong, blame Joe Murray. I'm beginning to think someone's decided I'm the national whipping boy."

Up ahead, amongst the cars parked facing the sea, Joe watched two men engaged in an argument. It took a moment to recognise them as the bearded individual who confronted Turgot in the hotel, and facing him, the more athletic individual who had been at odds with the snooty manager when they first arrived. The second individual was clad in jeans and a bomber jacket, and close by was a large motorcycle. Joe and his friends neared them, the bomber jacket took a couple of steps towards the bike and picked up the helmet, ready to put it on. Arnholt followed him.

"He's got an attitude problem, that beard."

"It's nothing to do with us, Joe." Brenda checked her

watch. "Keep out of it and let's get a cup of tea."

As they passed the two men, neither gave them a passing glance, but Joe caught part of the argument.

"I'm nearly broke, man. I need more money."

"Rose controls the cash, not me. I only advise her and the fact is, we don't have it. And let's face it, you're not good enough on the horn to go elsewhere, are you?"

"At least I know where I could stick the slide on your trombone."

The argument dissolved into the background sound of a seaside town as Joe and his friends went on their way. Out on the sands, close to the pier, gulls were out in force, circling low, their sharp eyes ever open on the lookout for discarded morsels of food, or the opportunity to steal an ice cream cone from unsuspecting hands. The wind was lighter but chilly, and overall, the three were glad to get into a small, bright café opposite the pier.

While the women seated themselves, Joe went to the counter, ordered two cups of tea and cakes.

"You know, I first came to Cleethorpes when I was a kid, a good fifty years ago, and the tide was out then."

The assistant smiled. "You called it right, then. It's due back in any time now."

She giggled and Joe pulled a face. "Yes, very funny."

She handed over his change. "People are always saying how the tide doesn't come in at Cleethorpes, but it does, you know. All the way up to the sea wall. Not very deep, but it does come in."

Joe pocketed his change and picked up the tray of food and drink. "We're here for the weekend, so I'll keep an eye open for it."

Joe joined the two women, distributed the cups, and left the tray of cakes in the middle of the table.

Picking up a maid of honour and biting into it, Brenda chewed, washed the mouthful down with a swig of tea, and asked, "Who was that awful man in the hotel and on the front just now?"

"They were both band members," Sheila said. "Didn't you

hear them mention a horn and a slide trombone?"

"Paul Caswell and Campbell Arnholt," Joe declared, and laughed as their surprised eyes fell upon him. "You looked at the board in reception, Brenda. They were both on there."

"You have a remarkable memory for trivia."

"Attention to detail is what it is."

Sheila stepped in to avert the inevitable ribald comments. "Well, let's hope they've settled their differences before tonight's performance."

From the seafront, they made their slow way up into the town centre. Slow because it involved walking up a short but steep hill away from the promenade, a climb which Joe found arduous.

"Didn't Mort say there were no hills in Cleethorpes?"

"He was working from memory, Joe," Sheila insisted.

"Yeah, but was his memory firing on all cylinders?"

By the time they reached the top, Joe was compelled to sit on a low wall close to a row of bus stops, and take a couple of puffs on his inhaler. No sooner had he put the device back in his pocket than he took out his tobacco tin and rolled a cigarette.

Brenda disapproved. "I have never seen anything so stupid. You struggled to breathe coming up that hill and when you get to the top, you take a shot from your inhaler and then light up."

"The smoke makes me cough, and I need to cough up the crap, it helps my breathing."

Sheila, too, remonstrated. "It would help your breathing more if you gave up that disgusting habit."

"And it'd help your bank balance if you gave up chucking money around in expensive shops. Do I complain about your retail therapy?"

"All the time."

"Especially when you have to carry it for us."

"Pack mule. That's what I am."

Joe gave up the unequal argument and lit his cigarette, prompting another coughing fit before he was able to carry on.

The town's shopping area consisted of a single street,

littered with shops of all shapes, sizes and descriptions on both sides, many of them familiar, High Street names. While Sheila and Brenda homed in on the clothing stores, Joe found a bench further down the street, alongside the entrance to a small, shoppers' car park, and finished his cigarette.

As always, when waiting for his two friends, he allowed his mind to wander, until it finally settled on the argument between Caswell and Arnholt. To him it sounded as if Arnholt was seeking a pay rise and Caswell refused to play ball, and that begged the question, what was the ranking situation between the two men? Caswell insisted that the woman, Rose, whom Joe, once more recalling the advertising board in the hotel entrance, identified as Rose Louden, controlled the money, but Arnholt – if Joe read the argument correctly – must have some kind of leading status, or how could he be asking for more money?

It was the kind of academic, mental exercise, which kept Joe's mind sharp, alert, a vital attribute to his infrequent adventures as a private investigator. It was his proud boast that nothing escaped Joe Murray's attention, and he had demonstrated as much when he pointed out to his friends that he recognised both men from that same poster in the hotel lobby.

When, therefore, he saw a powerful motorcycle coming down the street with a pillion passenger behind the rider, he recognised not the bike but the bomber jacket as Caswell's. And that was before he came to a stop in front of the Sunbeam Guest House and took off his helmet. Biker's leathers did nothing to disguise the fact that his passenger was a woman. Joe was amazed by the speed at which Caswell must have moved. Less than half an hour ago he was arguing with Arnholt on the seafront, and there was no sign of a woman nearby, and yet, here he was turning up with one.

His thinking cleared when she, too, removed her helmet, and Joe recognised her as Rose Louden. According to that same advertising board, the band was led by Tommy Louden. Her husband? Or her brother? If it was her husband, then the Shoreline Swingsters had more problems than Arnholt's demands for a pay rise. And if Tommy Louden was, as the board claimed, the band's leader, how come Arnholt was asking Caswell for a pay rise and how come Caswell claimed Rose was responsible for money?

The questions became even more compelling when Caswell and Rose disappeared into the bed & breakfast.

From Turgot's response to Arnholt it was reasonable to assume that although the band was the resident entertainment, the term was not meant to be taken literally. They did not reside in the Queen Elizabeth Hotel. So were they all staying at the B&B opposite, or did Caswell and Rose have something more secretive and entertaining in mind?

None of it was any of Joe's business, but he slotted the various bits and pieces into an empty filing cabinet in his mind, which he then labelled, Cleethorpes Shoreline Swingsters.

When Sheila and Brenda joined him, they took a taxi back to the hotel, and Joe was surprised how short the journey was. He'd calculated it at about a mile, but in fact it was less than half that distance. He and the women parted company on the third floor, agreeing to meet in the dining room at seven.

His room was small but comfortably warm, and unlike many of the seaside hotels they had visited, the furnishings were comparatively modern. The single bed was on legs, not castors, the headboard fixed to the wall, and the single wardrobe had ample room for his clothing and small suitcase. The en-suite bathroom, where white tiling and chrome fittings gleamed in the halogen lighting, rivalled many of the foreign hotels they had stayed in, and all in all, it was well worth the money they had paid.

Joe took out his clothing for the evening, then laid out his shaving gear in the bathroom, and satisfied that he was set up to get ready for a night of entertainment, he kicked off his shoes, threw himself onto the bed, and minutes later, he was asleep.

\*\*\*

At home, Joe's alarm clock was set permanently for 4:45 a.m. but it was rare that he needed it. He awoke almost automatically five or ten minutes before it went off. Here in Cleethorpes, he set the alarm on his smartphone for six p.m. but was woken at half past five by an insistent knocking on his door.

Muttering curses, he rolled from the bed, dropped his feet into a pair of loafers, stood up, and glanced through the window. The sun had not quite set (it would not go down for another half-hour or more according to his phone) and the rooftops behind the hotel were bathed in a harsh, crimson glow.

More hammering on the door. "All right, all right, I'm coming."

He had been dreaming but he could not recall the content of the dream. Probably something to do with The Lazy Luncheonette. It usually was, and as always, when waking up in that stage of sleep, he felt irritable and groggy as he walked to the door.

Brenda was about to knock again when he opened it.

"Joe, we have an emergency."

His senses began to coalesce. "What? What emergency?"

"Mort Norris. He's disappeared."

Joe's tired face screwed up into a mask of mystery. "Mort? What do you mean disappeared?"

"For crying out loud, Joe, I'm talking simple English. Mort has gone missing. Mavis Barker and Cyril Peck raised the alarm, and right now, Les Tanner's holding court with Alma in the bar. We could do with you down there. If nothing else, you know how to calm people down. All Les can do is make a note of the people down there and arrange them in alphabetical order."

Joe groaned. "Okay. Give me a minute, and I'll be down there."

He closed the door, moved to the bathroom, where he swilled off in cold water, decided he would skip the shave for the evening, and changed his clothing, discarding his denim jeans, pulling on a pair of fawn, casual trousers, and a thick, but short-sleeved shirt, and topped it with his ubiquitous gilet. Ensuring the pockets were fully loaded with Ventolin inhaler, wallet, tobacco, and lighter, he left the room and made his way down to the bar where, as Brenda promised, a significant group of Sanford's 3rd-agers were gathered.

Les Tanner greeted him cynically. "Ah. Here comes our chairman. We have a problem, Murray."

"So I've been told. What's this about Mort?"

Tanner aimed a gentle finger at Alma who in turn pointed at Mavis Barker and Cyril Peck and announced, "They're saying Mort has gone walkabout."

Mavis Barker took up the story. "Me and Cyril saw him in a pub in the town. He was coming out as we went in. We said hello, and said we'd see him back here. He said 'I won't be there' and he left the pub. While me and Cyril thought he just had a mood on him, when we looked out the window, he was getting on a bus."

Joe fumed. "And you dragged me out of bed for that? Maybe he couldn't be bothered walking back here."

Mavis returned Joe's scowl. "The bus was going to Grimsby."

Joe turned to Alma. "Are you worried?"

She shook her head. "Not yet. He often goes out on his own. I meanersay, Joe, his life is all work and looking after me. He's entitled to a bit of freedom."

Joe swung back to Mavis and Cyril. "There y'are. Maybe he fancies a few beers near the fish dock. For God's sake, he's fifty odd years old, he can come and go as he pleases, and if Alma's not bothered—"

"You didn't see him, Joe," Cyril interrupted. "He looked… I dunno… As if he was in another world."

"Worried?"

"Well, I wouldn't say worried, but certainly not with it."

Joe let out an exasperated sigh. "Well, I don't know what you expect me to do? All I can say to all of you is keep an eye out for him. If you spot him, let us know. Better yet, let Alma know. Now if no one minds, I'm going outside for a smoke."

# Chapter Five

There was a bench immediately outside and to the left of the entrance. Stepping out into the dying embers of the afternoon, Joe found Alec Staines enjoying a cigarette, and joined him.

"All right, Joe?"

Joe took out his tobacco tin and rolling machine, and began to put together a cigarette. "I was until that lot started on about Mort."

Alec chuckled. "I'd heard. Happen Mort has something going down in Grimsby."

"Alma doesn't appear to be bothered, but according to the members it's not allowed." Joe concentrated on the cigarette, removing it from the machine, and as he did so, he changed the subject. "Good hotel."

Alec agreed. "Not a bad little place, for sure."

"We've travelled further and fared worse."

Like Sheila, like Brenda, Alec had been a friend since the days of the schoolyard, and Joe had always insisted that had Alec's wife, Julia, not chosen her painter and decorator husband, Joe would have pressed her to become the first Mrs Murray. They were a handsome couple. Julia had aged well, and was still a spectacularly good-looking woman while Alec's job – like Joe's – kept him fit and active. Along with George Robson and his buddy Owen Frickley, and the Tanner-Goodson duo, the Staineses had been founder members of the 3rd Age Club, and it was rare that they missed an outing or excursion.

"How's your Wes doing these days? Still raking it in up in the Lake District?"

Alec puffed contentedly on his cigarette. "Making money

hand over fist, so he tells us. Oh and Kelly's pregnant. Due late summer." He chuckled. "Making me a granddad before my time."

"Gar, pull the other one. You'll spoil the kid rotten."

"Well. Julia's making plans for more visits to Windermere come August and September." Alec turned to look at Joe. "You never had kids, did you? You and Alison?"

Joe sighed and put a light to his cigarette. "Blessing in disguise, I think, because I don't know that it would have made any difference to the way things turned out. It wasn't marriage that put Ali off. It was the café. All work and no time off. You know the script. You've been self-employed practically all your working life."

"True, but I don't live on the job, Joe. I work in other peoples' houses, kitchens and offices don't I?"

Joe gazed out across the sands, slowly melding into the coming darkness. He brought the debate back to Alec's original prompt. "I have Lee, you know. He's like a son to me. I virtually brought him up, if you remember. I know he's thick as a brick, but he's a good-hearted lad. And talking of Lee, if you need a christening cake for the kid, have a word with him. He'll do you one at cost, and he's a brilliant cook, you know. It'd be good for him to have a challenge. Something other than full English breakfasts for the brewery drivers."

"I'll bear it in mind."

They lapsed into contemplative silence. Joe stared straight ahead, through the sparse trees of Pier Gardens, to the sands and sea beyond, where a container ship, its hull bathed in the dying embers of the day, made its way out to the North Sea.

"How's Julia?"

"Same as, Joe, same as." Alec crushed out his cigarette in the nearby stubber, took out another and lit it. "She likes her breaks from routine does our lass. Holidays abroad, the 3rd Age Club do's. She says it's what life's all about." He laughed. "It's also what working twenty-four-seven is all about. Making sure we can afford it."

Following Alec's lead, Joe crushed out his cigarette

underfoot, picked up the stub and dropped it in the ashtray beneath the stubber, then resumed his seat and began to roll another.

The unexpected blaze of a single headlight and the growl of a motorcycle engine assailed them. Paul Caswell's machine turned into the drive, followed by a Range Rover. They parked opposite the bench. Caswell climbed from his machine and removed his helmet. Alongside him, Tommy and Rose Louden, both wrapped in topcoats, beneath the hem of which, Rose's full-length, spangled gown could be seen.

Caswell gave them a smile. "Looking forward to the show, oldies?"

With memories of the elderly Sir Douglas Ballantyne's passion for heavy metal music at the forefront of his mind, Joe smiled back. "I don't know. Do you do much Black Sabbath?"

Caswell laughed. "Never give up hope, grandad." He turned to the other two band members. "We better use the side entrance. Tuna fish was getting out of his pram earlier."

Amused by Caswell's disrespect for their advancing age, puzzled at his reference to the manager as 'tuna fish', while impressed by his complete disregard for Turgot's inherent snobbery, Joe and Alec watched them disappear around the side of the building.

"Interesting," Joe said.

"Smartarse, you mean."

"No, not Caswell's idiocy. Earlier today I saw him and the blonde disappearing into a bed-and-breakfast in the middle of Cleethorpes. But I didn't see any sign of that Range Rover."

Alec laughed. "Are you suggesting something naughty's going on?"

"No. I'm making an observation. It's entirely up to the individual what conclusions they draw from it."

Alec crushed out his second cigarette and checked his watch. "Almost time for dinner. I'd better go find she who must be obeyed. Catch you later, Joe."

Joe was just a few minutes behind him, and met up with Sheila and Brenda as they were ready to enter the dining room. Sheila was, as always, dressed in dark, sombre colours, a navy blue skirt, with a matching top, bedecked with brooches and other items of paste jewellery. Brenda wore a shorter skirt in maroon, topped with a white blouse, the upper buttons left open. Both women wore high heels, which left Joe, usually the same height as them, inferior by a couple of inches.

Joe opted for fruit juice as a starter, followed by a pork steak and vegetables, while the two women chose melon slices to start, and beef risotto for the main course. Meals were included in the price, but drinks were not, and while Joe asked for a glass of beer with his meal, the women shared a half bottle of house red.

The dining room hummed to the clatter of knife and fork, and the rhubarb murmur of background conversation, and occasionally, they were able to pick out the voices of one or other of their members. It was a satisfied and satisfying orchestration to what was an excellent, well prepared and well-served meal, and throughout, Joe, Sheila and Brenda kept their conversation general, in keeping with the holiday mood, and there was no mention of The Lazy Luncheonette, and only the occasional passing reference to Sanford.

Joe declined dessert, finished off his beer, and left the dining room to step outside for an after-dinner smoke. On the same bench he had occupied earlier, he found Les Tanner puffing contentedly on his pipe.

"Not often I say this, Murray, but you've done us proud this time."

Joe busied himself rolling a cigarette. "When have I ever let you down, Les?"

"You want me to give you an itemised list?"

The superficial antipathy between the two men was not as serious as a casual observer might imagine. Tanner had been a part-time army officer for many years, and his employment status as the head of Payroll with Sanford Borough Council, led him to conclude that he was a much better administrator and organiser than Joe Murray would ever be, but it was noticeable that when Tanner took over the Chair of the 3rd

Age Club, the regimentation with which he approached every task made him unpopular, and despite his semi-jocular criticism of Joe, when he resigned the Chair, he was one of those signatories who put Joe forward for re-election.

"How Sylvia?"

"In fine form, thank you. It's the sea air, Joe. Does her the power of good, and she's really looking forward to the entertainment. She always enjoyed big band music."

Joe chuckled and lit his cigarette. "Small band music in this case. My mother loved it, you know. The Dorsey Brothers, Glenn Miller, Benny Goodman. Hangover from World War Two in her case. She reckoned Glenn Miller helped us win the war."

"Good for morale." Tanner abruptly changed the subject. "And what of Sheila and Brenda? Sheila in particular. Is she over the problems that swine caused?"

"I think so. She won't talk about it, you know, but she was at the hospital yesterday and there are no lingering after effects. When I think about things like that, Les, and other incidents in the past – Palmanova, for example – it drives home just how much the members support one another." Joe laughed. "Unless your name's Mort Norris."

"We wouldn't have sent for you if we weren't concerned, and that concern came from Mavis and Cyril's worries about him."

"But not Alma. It's no problem, Les. I was grouchy because Brenda woke me up. The least we can do is look out for Alma." He laughed again. "I remember I had you lot babysitting me in Palmanova, didn't I?"

"And according to Brenda, when you ran away, it was to draw that madwoman away from the other members. I had my doubts at the time, Joe, but both Sheila and the police backed up your story." Les knocked the dottle from his pipe. "Time I was getting back. I'll see you in the ballroom, maybe give you a lesson in how to dance properly."

Joe chuckled again. "I can do the twist."

Ten minutes later, with the time coming up to eight o'clock Joe followed Tanner's example and made for the ballroom. He was immediately impressed by its size – unbelievably large considering the overall amount of room the hotel didn't take up – and its organisation. Tables catering for up to six people were spaced around the perimeter of a large, polished dancefloor, and at the front, where the curtains were closed, stood a small stage where the Shoreline Swingsters would perform.

He found Sheila and Brenda stationed towards the rear left, not far from the bar, where a crowd, most of them Sanford 3rd-agers, had gathered. The women had obviously beaten the crush. A glass of beer stood in front of Joe's seat, while Sheila had a tall glass, probably a spritzer, if Joe knew anything about her, and Brenda entertained her favourite Campari and soda.

There was waiter service, and to Joe's surprise, one of those attendants was Vicky Ordish. It was an even greater surprise to find Turgot working behind the bar.

Brenda explained it. "We queried it, and he said they were short-handed. The season doesn't officially start until Easter."

Joe snorted. "What? And he couldn't get temps in? He's cutting back on costs. Paying that girl overtime is cheaper than bringing in agency labour. An ambitious man if you want my opinion. Trying to show the top management how efficient he can be. I'll bet his ambitions are a lot higher up the scale than Cleethorpes."

"Another famous Joe Murray deduction?" Sheila asked. "Like the time you believed Teri Goodson's boyfriend was guilty."

Joe recalled the case in Skegness, just down the coast from Cleethorpes. "I got it right eventually, didn't I?"

"Only after alienating the entire cast of Hamlet and the Lincolnshire police," Brenda reminded him.

"The cast of that particular farce deserved alienating," Joe responded. "In fact, it looked like it was written by an alien."

While speaking to the women, he cast an eye around the room and found himself impressed with Vicky's ability. He had classified her with the Lee Murrays and Kayleigh Watsons of this world. Eager, willing to work, but inherently clumsy, and yet as she wove her way through the tables she balanced her tray, often stacked with drinks, held high in one hand, reminding Joe of the bar waiters he had seen in many a European city.

A couple of minutes later, the lights dimmed and the PA system resounded to the voice of an announcer. "Ladies and gentlemen, the Queen Elizabeth Hotel proudly presents an evening with the Shoreline Swingsters."

Backed with a burst of music from piano, drums and double bass, the curtains parted, and spotlights picked out Rose Louden, fronting the band with an old-fashioned stand mike. She ran into *It Don't Mean a Thing (if it ain't got that swing)*.

Maintaining a degree of ambivalence, Joe assessed both the band and the audience reaction.

They were perfectly attired. The seven men wore royal blue blazers and light grey trousers, backed with dazzling white shirts and black ties bearing the band's logo, a complex arrangement of two capital letter S's interwoven and composed of gold (or a facsimile of same) thread.

As he suggested to Alec Staines earlier, they were too few in number to be described as a 'big band' but what they lacked in members, they more than made up for in volume. Rose's raucous voice filled the room, almost drowning out the sound of the backing instruments. The female pianist gave some verbal backing while hammering out the background theme. Beyond the basic three instruments of electronic piano, double bass and drums, there were two saxophones, two trumpets, Paul Caswell on trombone, and Tommy Louden, busily conducting the band, holding a clarinet in his free hand.

Within a few bars, the audience were lapping it up. For his part, Joe could take or leave it. Notwithstanding his jibe against Caswell, he preferred the music of the 1970s, Abba and the like, but he charitably accepted that this was preferable to the bland, sometimes incomprehensible music of today. Incomprehensible, he decided, purely as a factor of his age.

When Rose finished the number, she took a bow, and stepped back, giving the stage to her husband, Tommy.

"Well, good evening, ladies and gentlemen, and welcome to the Queen Elizabeth Hotel here in sunny Cleethorpes. The dancefloor's clear and only awaiting your feet. And just to get you tripping the light fantastic, here we go with Glenn Miller's *In The Mood*."

With Rose Louden now rattling away with a tambourine, the band ran into the lively introduction to one of Glenn Miller's best-known pieces, and almost immediately, Les Tanner and Sylvia Goodson, Mavis Barker and Cyril Peck took to the floor.

Sheila raised her eyebrows at Joe, who declined. "I'm not drunk enough yet."

As a result, Sheila and Brenda got up to dance. Alec and Julia Staines were not far behind them, and as Joe tapped his fingers and feet in time to the music, George Robson and Owen Frickley drained off their glasses, and made their way to the exit. Joe gave them a broad smile, and George returned a thumbs down.

The evening continued in the same, lively vein, while the Shoreline Swingsters concentrating mainly on Glenn Miller, diverged occasionally, churning out vocal numbers such as 'Do the Mess Around', 'Ain't Misbehaving', and even Ray Charles' 'What I Say'. At one point, Rose delivered her rendition of Patsy Cline's 'Crazy', which Joe equated more with a blurred line between country and pop, rather than swing.

From their Miller repertoire, they added 'String of Pearls' and 'Pennsylvania 65000', and as the time wore on, Joe, not drunk, but certainly brighter for his intake of ale, danced individually with Sheila and Brenda, both of whom congratulated him of his footwork.

"My mother taught me back in the days when we lived above the old café and she had nothing better to do with her time."

When, however, the band drifted into 'Moonlight Serenade' he declined again, without explanation this time. It had unfortunate memories for him. It was his mother's favourite, and an original recording of the tune played her in and out of the chapel during her funeral.

The Shoreline Swingsters called a twenty-minute interval at nine-fifteen, with the promise of another hour's entertainment to follow. Joe, having anticipated it, was one of the first at the bar, and had to wait while Turgot laid out a tray of drinks for the band. Many of them were clear, probably soft drinks, he guessed, but all were liberally iced and garnished with citrus fruits: slices of orange, lemon and lime. While Joe waited for another bartender to pour his beer and spirits for the two women, he overhead Turgot instructing Vicky, "The Tom Collins and the white wine spritzer look alike, so take care not to mix them up. Now go."

She had gone barely five yards when a loud crash prompted Turgot to begin mixing the drinks all over again, and Joe's mind was filled with images of Lee, smashed plates, baked beans, fried tomatoes, rashers of bacon, eggs and sausages splattered across the floor of The Lazy Luncheonette's kitchen. He instantly revised his earlier opinion of the girl.

He was still chuckling to himself when he related the tale to Sheila and Brenda. "It's nice to know you're not alone in the world of dealing with idiots."

They watched the progress of the band's drinks as Vicky delivered them – safely this time – to a small table, right of the stage. Rose Louden was first back in and after a brief word with Vicky, the waitress, pointed to a glass. Rose took it and stood it on the lectern from where her husband would conduct the band. Several minutes later, the rest of them began to drift back, and spent time sorting through the tray to take the drink of their choice. Tommy and Caswell were the last back, and as they took their drinks, it was time for the second set to begin.

Tommy took a sip from what looked like a glass of lemonade as he addressed the audience. "Time to get those feet moving again, ladies and gentlemen, and here's the beautiful Rose with her interpretation of Peggy Lee's smoochy classic… Fever."

The band ran into the introduction led by drums and double bass, with the remainder of the band clicking their fingers in time to the beat, and Rose, carrying a clear drink, ran into the lyric. It was a faithful rendition, and as she delivered the title word, Rose took a small sip from her glass. The grimace which followed might have been unnoticeable, it was so fast, but Joe spotted it before Rose could put a standard smile back on her features.

With thoughts of the overheard conversation at the bar, it occurred to Joe that Vicky must have mixed up the drinks.

A couple of minutes into the number, by which time the brass and piano were playing sharp, single notes to emphasise the staccato nature of the chorus, Paul Caswell, having taken a wet from his glass, began to cough. In deference to his fellow band members, he put down his trombone, backed off from the stand and moved away towards the exit, but before he reached it, he let out a strangled, guttural cry, and collapsed in a heap on the floor.

\*\*\*

Despite being on the wrong side of the ballroom, Joe was one of the first people to Caswell's assistance. He crouched on his haunches, loosened the man's shirt collar and tie, and with a crowd gathering around him, began to speak.

"Stay with me, buddy." He glanced around the crowd. "What's his name?"

Tommy Louden forced his way through. "Paul Caswell."

Joe returned to the younger man. "Paul. Try to keep calm, breathe normally, and try to focus when I speak to you."

All that came back was gargled nonsense.

Joe looked around the crowd again. "Anyone an experienced first aider?"

Louden gaped. "You mean you're not?"

"I know what I'm doing, but I'm not qualified. Now for God's sake someone find a first aider, and you," he nodded at Louden, "get back on the stand, and give this mob some music to keep them occupied." As Louden left, Turgot appeared, and Joe picked him out. "Call an ambulance."

"What gives you the right—"

"Stop arguing and dial 999. This man needs an ambulance."

"I—"

"Just do it. He swallowed something, and if we don't get the medics here soon, we don't know what'll happen."

Turgot disappeared and Julia Staines took his place. Joe frowned a question at her.

"I was a nurse, Joe. Remember? It might be years ago, but I still know what I'm doing."

"All right. It looked like he's swallowed something. He can't talk. All that comes out is garbage."

Now Julia frowned. "Standard procedure was to try and make them cough it up, but he looks bad, Joe. I don't know that we should be doing anything, other than keep him comfortable."

While she turned on the crowd, insisting that they disperse, Joe removed his gilet, folded it into a pillow shape and placed it under Caswell's head. Somewhere behind them, the band struck up Glenn Miller's Little Brown Jug, and Rose grabbed Les Tanner's arm, practically dragging him onto the floor and began to dance with him, while at the same time encouraging others to join them.

Joe concentrated on the patient. "Just take it easy, Paul. Help's on its way."

Caswell tried to swallow, and then spoke, but his voice was so distant, hoarse that Joe could not hear him.

"Say again."

Joe leaned his ear into Caswell's mouth, and caught an offensive stench from his outgoing breath.

"Spits."

Joe still could not hear properly, but that's what it sounded like.

Turgot reappeared. "Emergency ambulance on its way. Are you sure he's not just drunk?"

Joe was ready to turn on him, but Julia beat him to it. "Just get back behind the bar, Mr Turgot. Keep your drinkers occupied. Joe and I will look after him until the paramedics get here."

"May I remind you, Madam, that I run this hotel?"

Julia was more than equal to him. "You've done nothing but remind us since we got here. Now please, go away before I really take offence."

"One minute," Joe interrupted. "Turgot, how far is this ambulance coming?"

"About four miles. The Diana, Princess of Wales Hospital in Grimsby. They'll be here in a matter of minutes."

"Good. Then like Julia said, the best thing you can do is get back behind the bar and see to your customers."

With a distinct lack of grace, Turgot did as he was bidden, the dancefloor began to fill up and the crowd around the victim dispersed. Minutes later, the flashing blue lights of an emergency ambulance flickered on the windows, and soon after, a brace of paramedics appeared.

While one bent to tend Caswell, the other took details from Joe and Julia, including their names, room numbers, and relevant experience.

"I could smell something on his breath," Joe said. "Something I'm sure I'm familiar with, but I can't quite place it. The nearest I could come would be disinfectant, but it isn't, if you understand what I mean."

Within another fifteen minutes, Caswell was strapped onto a gurney and taken away to hospital, Julia returned to her husband, and Joe, relieved that the emergency was out of his hands, joined his two friends, who gave him a small, sympathetic round of applause.

"Thank God for Joe Murray," Sheila said.

Brenda was in complete support. "You deserve a reward, Joe. Shall I come to your room at midnight, or will we throw Sheila out and you can come to mine?"

"Too tired. Besides, I have Yvonne Naylor – pardon me – Vallance to think about."

Brenda laughed. "Dream on."

## Chapter Six

Karen Gipton yawned. Seven o'clock on a sunny but chilly Saturday morning in the middle of March would never find her at her best, especially when she had to leave the warmth and comfort of her semi-detached home south and slightly west of Grimsby town centre and drive to Cleethorpes. But that was the lot of a Detective Inspector.

Her sidekick, Detective Sergeant Melanie Watney, was a good deal younger than her, an ambitious young woman who would probably end up as Chief Constable one day in the distant future. Good luck to her was Karen's attitude. She had made DI and she was happy to remain there. At a pinch she might climb one more rung of the ladder, but she would need some serious persuasion.

Mel would make a good inspector, but for the moment she had a problem taking responsibility. Her call to Karen was a case in point.

"It's a suspicious death, boss," she said when she rang from the hospital. "He was brought into A & E just after ten last night, and they pronounced him dead an hour ago."

Just the bare details. That was Mel all over. Spare with information to the degree that Karen often had to drag it out of her.

"Identified?"

"Paul Caswell."

"Cause of death?"

"The hospital wouldn't commit one hundred percent, but they're confident that it was poisoning. Sodium hydroxide."

"Bleach?"

"Something like that, ma'am, and he swallowed it."

Karen tutted. "How? Where?"

"Queen Elizabeth Hotel, Cleethorpes. He was a member of the band appearing there."

Karen reached a decision. "All right, Mel. Get over there, kick-start the manager, and I'll be with you in, say, half an hour."

"Roger."

Karen left her husband snoring contentedly, jumped in the shower then dressed, gulped down a cup of coffee and climbed into her car for the three-mile, ten-minute journey to Cleethorpes Beach.

The sun, hidden behind the high density housing, rose half an hour previously and the sky was clear of cloud. If the wind dropped, it would be a warm day, and that, in turn, meant crowds making for Cleethorpes Beach, right opposite the Queen Elizabeth, but the worst thing about working in a seaside town, was the hour traders opened up for business. In Grimsby, she could get a decent cuppa and bite to eat at this time, but in Cleethorpes, she'd be lucky to find anywhere open for at least another hour.

She pulled into the forecourt of the Queen Elizabeth a little after half past seven, to find Mel waiting for her. As she arrived, two men seated on a bench, smoking cigarettes, watched with interest. Karen ignored them and followed Mel into the hotel where they confronted a tired, yet immaculately turned out Turgot.

His surly attitude convinced Karen that he believed himself deserving of a superintendent's attention, rather than a common or garden inspector. His precise English and cultured tones dripped disdain.

"I told your sergeant that I was serving drinks behind the bar when the incident occurred, Inspector. I saw nothing. Indeed, I didn't realise anything had gone wrong until the band stopped playing and a crowd gathered at the ballroom exit, and when I got there, I was treated to the most disrespectful instructions… No, not instructions: orders from one of our guests."

"The guest in question being?"

"If you know anything about the law, Inspector, you'll

understand that our guests have a right to privacy, and it's not for me to—"

Already sick of his demeaning attitude, Karen cut him off. "Either tell me the guest's name, Mr Turgot, or I will charge you with obstructing the police in the course of their enquiries. And before you give us any more verbal diarrhoea, I will require a full list of everyone staying at the hotel, and don't tell me I need a warrant. This is a murder inquiry, and those guests may very well have vital evidence. I don't have time to fool around approaching magistrates for a warrant. Now, who was the guest who told you what to do."

"Joseph Murray. Room 307."

The name rang an instant bell with Karen. "Let me see your guest list."

"I'm not sure—"

Karen nodded to her sergeant, who understood, and intoned, "Armand Turgot, I'm arresting you for obstructing the police in the course of their enquiries. I must caution you—"

Turgot held up his hands in surrender, moved to the computer, opened up the registration screen, and turned the monitor to face the police.

Karen scanned the list, and without taking her eyes from it, said, "I'll need a full print out of this list. Not in ten minutes time, but now." She studied the list until she found the entry she was looking for. "I thought as much. Where is Murray now?"

Turgot, busy sending instructions to the printer, shrugged. "It's not my place to question guests on their whereabouts. However, I think you passed him on your way in. I believe he was making his way out to smoke one of those disgusting hand-rolled cigarettes he prefers."

Karen nodded. "Get me that print out. Mel; with me."

\*\*\*

Getting out of bed early was an integral part of Joe's life and ingrained in his system, but the consolation of a weekend break was that he could go back to bed and catch up on sleep any time he wished.

It was no surprise to see him up just before half past six on Saturday morning. Indeed, the surprise was that he had slept so late. Determined not to waste the time, he washed, shaved, dressed and then took himself downstairs and out of the hotel, where he perched on the bench by the entrance, rolled and lit his first cigarette of the day. It was followed, as it always was, by his first coughing fit of the day, and a rapid infusion of Ventolin from his inhaler.

"When will you learn, you bloody fool?"

"Put you away for talking to yourself, Joe," Alec Staines said as he came out of the hotel.

"And there are those who say it's the only way to make sense of this barmy world."

Alec sat alongside him, took out a cigarette, lit it, dropped his lighter back in a trouser pocket. As he did so, a saloon car pulled into the drive and parked opposite them. A woman climbed out and walked into the hotel where she was greeted by another woman who obviously knew her.

Alec's eyebrows rose. "Aye, aye; what's this then?"

Joe also watched the woman's progress, and he had seen the first woman in reception when he came down, where she had been in deep and serious conversation with Turgot.

"Police," he said.

Alec laughed. "How do you know?"

"Experience. That guy from the band last night. Someone obviously spiked his drink, and when he got to hospital, the first thing they'd do is call the police. Ten to one they spent half the night there waiting for him to come round and tell them what happened… if he could remember any of it. The next stop would be here."

"The famous Joe Murray deductive process."

Joe chuckled. "It's also handy having a niece who's a copper."

Alec drew on his cigarette. "You gonna poke your nose in?"

"Not likely. I've come here for a weekend off."

Breakfast was not served until half past eight and while Alec returned to his room after his smoke, Joe elected to stay where he was and wait for developments. He did not have long to wait before the two women stepped out of the hotel and confronted him.

"Is it Mr Murray?"

"That depends. If I owe you money, no. If you owe me money, then I'm him." He smiled to demonstrate that he was only joking.

Karen took out her warrant card. "DI Gipton, Humberside police. This is Detective Sergeant Watney. We're making inquiries into the incident with Paul Caswell last night, and according to the manager, Mr Turgot, you were quite, er, abrupt in taking control of the situation."

Joe puffed on his cigarette. "Turgot's a nit-picking pen pusher. He wanted an official first aider to look over the man, then fill in all the forms, and then he might have called for an ambulance. I insisted he dialled 999 straight away. And before you ask, no, I'm not a qualified first aider, but I had a lady with me, Julia Staines, who was a qualified nurse at one stage of her career. In other words, Ms Gipton, we knew what we were doing. That man needed urgent medical attention, not someone faffing about filling in bits of paper."

Karen took a seat next to him, Mel sat the other side and lit a cigarette while her boss took the lead.

"We're getting off on the wrong foot here, Mr Murray—"

"Please call me Joe. I've never been one for formality."

"Obviously. I'm Karen and this is Mel. Indulge me for a minute. About a year back I was on a course up in York and I met a DI Craddock from Sanford. She told me all about her, er, father, I think, who ran some sort of a café, manages a social club for the middle-aged and elderly, and was simply the best detective the police service had never seen." Karen smiled generously. "Your daughter?"

"My niece," Joe corrected her. "Gemma always was one for flattery… especially when I'm out of earshot."

"She says you have exceptional powers of observation."

"When she's with me, she tells me I'm nosy." He took

another drag on his cigarette. "Forgive me, Karen, but is this leading somewhere?"

"I shouldn't really tell you, but Paul Caswell died a couple of hours ago."

Joe buried his immediate shock. "And you think I hastened his death?"

"Nothing of the kind. I'm sure you and Ms… Staines, was it? I'm sure you and she did all you could before the paramedics arrived. I'm more interested in your niece's claims regarding your powers of observation. If she's right, you probably noticed an awful lot more than you've said to anyone. What can you tell me?"

Joe's cigarette had gone out. It was part and parcel of hand-rolling them. He dug into his gilet, pulled out his lighter and lit it again. Dropping the lighter back in his pocket, he said, "There was a smell. I know I should recognise it, but I couldn't quite place it. Something like disinfectant, but not disinfectant."

Karen raised her eyebrows at Mel.

"According to the hospital he was poisoned by household bleach."

Joe snapped his fingers. "That's it. That's what I could smell on his breath. Bleach mixed with booze."

When Karen responded to him, it was with an air of caution. "That's not an official diagnosis, Joe. When Mel spoke to them this morning, they refused to commit one hundred percent until they've carried out the necessary tests. I have a problem with this. How did bleach get into his drink? And how come he drank it without noticing? I mean, when he lifted the glass to his lips, he must have smelt it."

"Smelled," Joe corrected her. "Smelt is the run-off from molten iron, or it could be a fish." He grinned at her. "I know it's old-fashioned, but so am I."

Karen returned the smile. "Aside from correcting my English with even more iffy English, you didn't answer my question."

Joe's brow knitted in concentration, straining to recall the sequence of events of the previous evening.

"I can only tell you what I saw. Turgot, the snobby manager, was working behind the bar and he prepared drinks for the band, all ten of them. He gave them to the waitress, a young lass named Vicky... Sorry, I can't remember her surname. It was an interval and the bar was crowded. I don't think she got further than a few yards before she dropped the bloody lot, and had to come back. Turgot was getting more frustrated by the minute, and he set up a second lot of drinks. By the time the girl delivered them to the band's table, they were due back on stage... in fact, Rose Louden was already back. I saw her talking to Vicky. Next thing, they were all taking their glasses up and taking up their positions. They went into their next number, which involved a lot of finger-snapping from the band. I didn't see it personally, but five'll get you ten that Caswell took a quick slurp while he was snapping his fingers. Then, he started coughing, and came off stage, making for the exit. Logical thing to do, I suppose. He probably imagined he needed a breath of fresh air. He never made it. He collapsed in the doorway. The band stopped playing, and I legged it over there to see how I could help."

Karen waited until Mel brought her notes up-to-date, and then congratulated Joe. "A detailed account. That's what we like. Now, the question: did you see anyone tampering with the drinks?"

"No. I mean, I'm here for a weekend break and I wasn't paying that much attention. The band came back in ones and twos, so I suppose any of them could have spiked the drink, and obviously, Turgot and the waitress could have done, too. Especially Turgot. He'd had hassle with Caswell when we first arrived, and then a bit later, he had more hassle from the trumpet player. Big bugger. Campbell Arnholt, I think he's called."

"How do you mean hassle?"

Joe's frown deepened. "Again, I wasn't taking that much notice, but from all I gather, Caswell and Arnholt came into the front entrance and they're not supposed to. Last night, me and one of our members were having a smoke when Caswell turned up on his motorbike, and the Loudens were right behind him in their Range Rover. Caswell was saying how they had to use the side entrance because Turgot was getting his hair off earlier in the day over them using the front door."

"And did Caswell appear concerned over Turgot's annoyance?"

"Anything but." Joe chuckled and reached behind to stub out his cigarette. "I didn't know the bloke, but he struck me as one of those men who really don't give a stuff about anyone."

"Well at least you're giving us something—"

Joe cut her off. "There's a bit more you should know." He waited until she nodded for him to go on. "Yesterday afternoon, my friends and I were walking along the seafront when we passed Caswell and Arnholt, and they were arguing, about money. Arnholt wanted a pay rise. At least, that's what it sounded like. Caswell said the band couldn't afford it and anyway pay was not part of his remit. That was down to Rose Louden. And talking of Rose, my friends were shopping on the main street during the day, and I saw Caswell and Rose turn up at the Sunbeam Guest House on his motorcycle. Now, I don't wanna cast aspersions, but I didn't see Tommy Louden's Range Rover anywhere nearby. I'll leave you to draw your own conclusions."

"You suspect an affair?"

"If not, it's certainly open to that kind of interpretation. On the other hand, it could be perfectly innocent. It Caswell was telling it right when he spoke to Arnholt, then it's reasonable to assume that Caswell felt it necessary to pass the information onto Rose who apparently controls the money. My only question would be, why meet in that guest house?"

Mel nodded her agreement. "Most murders are about sex or money, aren't they, guv?"

"Which is something we'll bear in mind." Karen focused on her sergeant. "Have you got everything?" When Mel replied with a nod, Karen switched her attention back to Joe. "Thanks for your help. If you can think of anything else, don't hesitate to let us know." She reached into her pocket and came out with a business card which she handed to him.

By return, Joe took out a pocket notebook and scribbled down his mobile number. "If you need me, that's the number. I leave it on twenty-four-seven."

Karen took the note and laughed. "Your niece was right about you. She said you can't resist shoving your nose in."

"That's our Gemma. My favourite niece. Right now, I'm going to shove my nose into breakfast."

## Chapter Seven

In common with most hotels, breakfast was self-service, and when Joe stepped into the dining room at twenty past eight, he found a huge queue, comprised mostly of his members shuffling along.

It was just after half past eight, when he finally joined Sheila and Brenda at a window table where Joe, disappointed that the view was to the side and not the front of the hotel, robbing him of the opportunity to follow the activity of the big, wide world across the road and on the seafront, tucked into an adequate full English breakfast, Sheila indulged her preference for muesli followed by toast and butter, and Brenda chose grapefruit, with toast to follow.

"Where have you been, Joe?" Brenda demanded.

"Talking with the cops outside."

"About last night?" Sheila wanted to know.

Joe nodded and chewed on a rubbery, Lincolnshire sausage. "If we served garbage like this, the draymen would be queueing up at Sid Snetterton's place."

"Not at the moment, they wouldn't. He's gone to the Bahamas with his wife."

Joe scowled. "So I heard. How come he gets the Bahamas and all we get—"

Brenda cut him off. "Last night, Joe?"

He took a swallow of tea. "Bad news. That lad, Caswell, he died in the early hours of this morning. According to the filth, he swallowed bleach."

Sheila gaped. Brenda was more philosophical. "The soda water in my Campari tasted a bit like Fairy Liquid, but I didn't think it was that bad."

It was as if the shock of his announcement had not sunk in,

and Joe glowered. "He's dead, Brenda. He was poisoned."

"Well, pardon me for breathing, but quite frankly, Joe, we have more important things to worry about than some dead trumpeter."

"Trombonist," Joe corrected her. "And what more important things?"

Brenda returned to her toast and nodded to Sheila, who took up the tale.

"Mort Norris. He didn't come back last night."

A forkful of stringy bacon and soggy egg white halfway between plate and his mouth, Joe stared. "You're sure?"

"Mavis told us first thing this morning."

Joe chewed on the food. "Mavis? Not Alma?"

Finished with her grapefruit, Brenda pushed the dish into the centre of the table. "According to Mavis… Oh. Here she is. Let her tell you."

Joe half turned to find Mavis waddling towards them. She stood over him. "You've heard about Mort?"

"Sheila and Brenda were just telling me. How's Alma?"

"Me and Cyril are looking after her. She says she's not bothered, but it's just a front. She's as worried as the rest of us."

"And has it occurred to any of you that he might just have got tanked up and crashed in the bus station or something?"

Mavis laughed. "Mort? Tanked up? Come off it, Joe."

"All right, then. Has it crossed your tiny mind that he might have a bit on the side?"

"I think that might be what's on Alma's mind. Joe, you've got to find him."

Brenda intervened. "Joe's on the case, Mavis. We'll keep you informed."

Mavis wandered away and Joe returned to his meal. "I'll find him if I can find the time."

"Now, Joe, he's a friend and a fellow club member. We—"

Joe cut Brenda off. "What's the score for this morning, then?"

The speed at which he interrupted telegraphed his intention not to discuss Mort and Alma Norris, and Sheila took the hint.

"Grimsby?" she asked. "I'm told there's some excellent shopping in, er, Freshley."

"Freshney." Joe munched through a piece of barely warm bacon. "Freshney Place. It's a shopping mall. A bit like Galleries in Sanford."

"Only ten times the size," Brenda added.

"Giving you the opportunity to spend ten times as much."

"Tightwad."

"I deny that. I'm engaged in a research study." While the women gaped, Joe swallowed the last of the bacon and egg. "They say that when you die, you can't take it with you, but I'm working on it."

He grinned, they groaned.

"Ignoring your idiotic comment, how do you know about Freshney Place?"

He put down his knife and fork, pushed the plate away, and helped himself to a second cup of tea from the pot. "It's called research, Sheila. See, I know you two. You're shopaholics. Between you, you have more designer clobber than a mail order catalogue model, and more shoes than Imelda Marcos. So I read up on it before—"

"Ladies and gentlemen, may I have your attention please?"

The female voice calling across the dining room silenced Joe and everyone else. All eyes turned to the entrance where Karen Gipton and Mel Watney stood.

"I'm Detective Inspector Gipton, Grimsby CID, and I apologise for interrupting your meal, but is Ms Julia Staines here?"

Everyone but Joe was surprised to hear Julia's name called out, and most of the eyes in the room, especially those belonging to the 3rd Age Club, turned in her direction when she half stood

"Hey up, Julia, have you been hawking it round Cleethorpes?"

A ripple of laughter ran through the room, and Joe scowled at George Robson. "Shut up, barmpot."

While he was remonstrating with George, an embarrassed Julia spoke up. "I'm Mrs Staines."

"There's nothing to worry about, Mrs Staines, but I'd be grateful if you could spare us a few minutes…" Karen gazed around the room. "…in private."

This time it was the elderly Irene Pyecock with the risible comment. "You should be careful getting up close and private with the Staineses, lass. You'll end up having your back bedroom wallpapered."

As Julia made her way to the exit, followed by her husband, the comments came thick and fast.

"Deny everything, Julia."

"Name, rank, and serial number only."

"Watch out for wet towelling in the cells."

"Insist on dry."

"We'll send you a cake with a file in it."

"And a hammer drill to get through the cake."

The good-natured repartee told Joe something about the camaraderie between these people, a generous crowd he was pleased to be a part of. None of them would see a member in trouble, and at the first sign of problems, they would rally round and do whatever they could to help.

"Is that about last night?" Brenda asked.

Joe nodded. "Probably. She did help me with Caswell at the door, and I did give them her name."

"It's also a good few years since she renewed her nursing licence," Sheila pointed out. "From a legal standpoint neither of you were qualified in first aid and you could both be in trouble for attending to that man."

Brenda rubbed it in. "Even worse, Joe, you could also be in trouble for complaining about the tide yesterday. For all we know this part of Humberside might be a totalitarian mini-state."

Taking their ribbing in good part, Joe suggested, "Fifty lashes with the cat?"

Brenda sighed. "I feel sorry for the cat already."

\*\*\*

Joe had to wait for Sheila and Brenda, and he once again

stepped outside to stock up his nicotine levels. He found Rose Louden on the bench, raised an eyebrow seeking permission, and when she nodded, he joined her.

This was a different Rose to the one who had entertained them the previous evening. She was dressed in jeans and a warm coat, wore no make-up, and the sparkle in her silver/blue eyes was gone. The death of Caswell probably hit the whole band, but Joe's sighting of her making her way into the Sunbeam Guest House suggested that it had hit her a lot harder than her fellow artistes, and putting aside the rights and wrongs of her potential adultery, Joe could identify with her pain. Hadn't Denise been taken from him in unexpected and violent circumstances?

"How are you this morning?"

She sniffed. "You must have heard about Paul?" She waited for him to silently confirm. "Then you can guess how I am."

Joe felt his temper igniting. No matter how deep her sense of loss, there was no excuse for rudeness. He brought his irritation under control. "It's always a shock. I know. I've been there."

"You think so? Somehow, I doubt it."

Joe fussed over lighting his cigarette. "My partner was murdered a couple of years ago."

Rose's reaction took him by surprise. He anticipated at least a sign of sympathy. What he got was a harsh laugh.

"Your partner was murdered? And that's the same as someone threatening your life, is it?"

Joe frowned. What on earth was the woman talking about? "I don't understand."

She faced him, her eyes burning into him. "That dumb waitress pointed out the wrong drink. I got the Tom Collins, he picked up my spritzer. That bleach was meant for me."

Joe snapped his fingers. That was what Caswell had been trying to say. Not 'spit' but 'spritzer'.

Rose flounced to her feet, and would have hurried into the hotel had Joe not stopped her. "Just a minute. Sit down, will you?"

She regained her seat, and he re-ran the chain of events

through his mind. Rose was singing, she picked up the glass, took a sip and screwed up her face. It was a fleeting moment, but one he recalled as if it had happened only a few moments ago. Anyone could be forgiven for thinking that she had picked up a glass tainted with bleach.

"Your man is dead, and yet you are saying it was intended for you. Have you told the police?"

"No. I'll deal with it myself."

"You're that tough are you?"

"A lot tougher than you might imagine."

"I don't know about that, but how many times in your life have you confronted a killer?"

Her lip curled again. "How many times have you?"

"I don't think you can count that far." This time, Joe's insult was deliberate. "Why would anyone want to shuffle you off?"

She shrugged. "There are reasons. None of your business."

"You mean someone who knew you were jumping Caswell?"

He said it with the express intention of shocking her, but once again she laughed. "Proper little smartarse, aren't you? I don't know who told you, but—"

Joe interrupted. "No one. I saw you yesterday, you and Caswell going into the Sunbeam Guest House, and I figured you weren't up for a game of Scrabble."

The needle struck home this time. "Has anyone ever told you to mind your own business?"

"Plenty of times. I ignored them. And if you tell me, I'll ignore you. I'm a private investigator… of sorts, and the police have already asked me to keep my ear to the ground. For crying out loud, woman, a man is dead, and it's odds on that the killer was a member of your crew. All right, it's possible that it could have been one of the hotel staff, but then you have to ask what kind of motive these people would have. How long have you been in residence here?"

"Er, let me see, it must be all of… one day." She could see her answer perplexed him, and laughed for a third time. "Tommy, Paul, and me, we were here in January to suss the place out. As a band, we've been here for a few weeks, rehearsing, but last night's performance was the first. If you want to look at the staff, be my guest, but you had it right the first time. It's more likely to be one of the band, and there could be any number of candidates."

"Including your husband?"

She hesitated before answering. "Including my husband."

\*\*\*

With no sign of Sheila or Brenda, Joe stepped back into the hotel and was surprised to find Alma Norris at reception. Not that it was a surprise to find her there, but she was out of her wheelchair.

He stood a respectful distance from her and Turgot, waiting until she had concluded whatever business she had with him, and as she turned away, hobbling to her wheelchair, he approached her.

She groaned. "Not you too, Joe. Why don't you people go away and leave me alone?"

"Mavis is pestering us. I just thought—"

"Outside for a smoke."

Alma did not wait for him to comment, but returned to her wheelchair, and steered the machine to the exit. By the time Joe caught up, she was outside, parked alongside the bench.

Rose Louden had left, so Joe took the empty seat, and while Alma lit a cigarette, he rolled one.

"Smoking when you have multiple sclerosis? Are you supposed to do that?"

With all the guile of the slyest fox, Alma threw the query back at him. "Smoking when you have COPD? Are you supposed to do that?"

"Touché."

Joe lit his cigarette and contemplated his approach. It did not need much thinking about. Alma was like him; outspoken, to the point.

"Mort didn't come back last night."

"Yes. And?"

"It doesn't bother you?"

"Why should it?"

Joe sighed. "You know, blood out of a stone is child's play compared to getting information from you. He's your husband, Alma, and your carer. Yet you're not bothered that he never came back to the hotel last night?"

"No. I told you yesterday, Joe, his life is work, work, work and looking after me. I let him slip the leash whenever I can, and I'm not totally bound to this bloody thing." She jabbed the arm of her wheelchair to indicate the 'bloody thing' in question. "I have what they call mobility issues, but I'm not completely crippled. Not yet. But I do need a lot of looking after, and Mort's entitled to some life."

The scenario running through Joe's mind was not conducive to gentle questioning, and he had no wish to upset Alma. "We're on our way to Grimsby. Would you like to come with us?"

"Not bloody likely. I was the one who suggested Cleethorpes to Mort so he could put it to the meeting in January, and I wanted Cleethorpes for a reason." With a long strand of ash hanging dangerously from her cigarette, she waved a hand at the North Sea and the ash fell, drifting slightly on the light wind, leaving a dusting of grey on the wheelchair arm. "The seaside," she went on. "I just want to sit here and remember this place from when I was a kid."

"Alone? You're content to be on your own, only—"

Alma laughed, a harsh, sarcastic bark. "Some chance. What with Mavis Barker hovering like a mother hen, and Cyril jumping to her every command." She sighed. "I keep telling them to go away, but they don't listen." She narrowed a cynical eye on him and took another pull on her cigarette. "A bit like you."

"It's called concern."

"Well, don't be concerned. I'm all right. And wherever he is, I'm sure Mort is too. You'll see. When he comes back – and he will come back – he'll be right as a bobbin. Whatever's going down with Mort is nothing to do with anyone but me and him. Now do us a favour, Joe. Bugger off to Grimsby and do like I'm trying to do. Enjoy yourself."

## Chapter Eight

Sheila sipped delicately from a cup of milky coffee. "You have this mental image of Grimsby as a sort of dour fishing town, the people dressed in oilskins, the women almost as hard-faced as the men, and a population struggling through what is a hard life. Even its name sounds cheerless: *Grim*-sby." She stressed the first syllable.

Brenda agreed. "People still have the same impression of Sanford, although not from its name. A town dominated by the pit and foundry." She waved vaguely through the windows of the cafeteria. "And yet, like Sanford, Grimsby's quite cosmopolitan."

Joe sneered. "I don't see many jet-setters touching base in Sanford… or Grimsby."

"Misery."

Beyond the small café was a wide open, pedestrianised square bathed in pleasant sunshine, and running alongside it, one of the main entrances to Freshney Place. It was half past ten, Saturday morning, and the weather had already tempted shoppers out, many of them clad in thin, summer wear, but just as many wearing an extra layer or two to fight off the light but nippy breeze.

On the periphery of their conversation, Joe, immersed in his thoughts, came to life. "It's the only serious, reasonably-sized centre of population for miles. Scunthorpe's what? Thirty miles away? Doncaster's fifty, and even if you cut across the Humber Bridge, I'll bet it's still forty miles to Hull. And besides, the state of the British fishing industry, they had to invest in other areas, even if it is retail."

Having said his piece, he sank once more into silence.

He had been noticeably quiet and thoughtful since his

meetings with the police and Rose Louden, and throughout the twenty minute bus journey from Cleethorpes Pier to the stands at Grimsby's Riverhead Exchange, outside Freshney Place Shopping Centre, he had barely said a word.

It was so unlike him that Sheila and Brenda commented upon it when he visited the toilets, and now, as he shut himself out again, Sheila tackled him.

"What is it, Joe? What did the police say to you? Is it Mort Norris?"

"What? No. I had a word with Alma before we left Cleethorpes, and she doesn't give a hoot about him staying out all night… or she says she doesn't, but we've known her a long time and when has she ever told it like it isn't? She might very well give Mort some stick when he comes back, but she as good as told me to mind my own business. To be truthful, I'm more interested in this band thing, Paul Caswell and the stuff Rose Louden told me."

The moment he said it, Joe wished he had not. Sheila and Brenda had years of experience to back them up, and keeping secrets from them was far more difficult than keeping them from MI6.

"What did Rose Louden tell you?"

When he did not immediately answer, Brenda stepped up the pressure. "Come on, Joe, this is us you're talking to, your best friends. You can tell us. And if you don't, I'll twist your arm up your back until you do."

"It's confidential."

"So's your bank account," Brenda insisted, "but I do your books and I know exactly how much you're worth, Joe Murray. I don't spread that about, do I? Course, I could let it slip. Accidentally, natch."

Joe glared daggers. "That's blackmail."

"I prefer to call it professional female persuasion."

He saw his opening. "So you're a professional female, are you? Funny. You've never given me a bill, have—"

"Joe." There was a dangerous edge to Brenda's voice.

"Will you two stop teasing each other?" Sheila drained her cup. "Now come on, Joe. You don't keep secrets from us two, and you know it. What's going on?"

He, too, finished his coffee and took out his tobacco tin to roll a cigarette. "What I'm gonna tell you is confidential... Well, Rose Louden insists she won't say anything to the cops, but I'm sure she'll have to at some stage. Caswell picked up the wrong drink last night. It was meant for Rose."

He gave them a few seconds to absorb the shocking news and then told them the rest of Rose's story.

Sheila was first to comment. "So the argument we saw on the seafront yesterday puts Arnholt in the frame, doesn't it? We heard Caswell tell him that Rose was in charge of money."

"Not necessarily." Joe went on to tell them what he had seen opposite Sunbeams in Cleethorpes, and the Loudens' arrival at the Queen Elizabeth the previous evening, and Caswell's comment regarding the hotel manager, Turgot.

"Just because you saw them, Joe—"

"She admitted they were having an affair," Joe interrupted before Brenda could go down the obvious route. "That's puts Tommy in the frame, if he knew about it, and the argument with Turgot puts him right in the frame."

Brenda finished her cappuccino, they got ready to leave, Joe settled the bill, and they stepped out into the sunny morning.

"It's a bog standard Joe Murray poke-your-nose-in affair then," Sheila said. "But why would Turgot aim for Rose?"

Joe shrugged. "Ask me another. Maybe he was aiming for Caswell and told young Vicky the drinks wrong. Told her the spritzer was the Tom Collins and vice versa. The girl is a bit slow, isn't she?"

Brenda hewed her lip. "Trouble is, Joe, we don't know anything about this band, or armband turbocharger, do we?"

"I didn't know anything about those idiots in Cornwall, did I? Or Tenerife? Or Whitby. But it didn't stop me."

Sheila considered this. "I'm sure there was something different about those cases, but I can't think what. This time, Joe, I think you'd be better concentrating on what happened to Mort Norris."

"And I told you, Mort is a free agent. He doesn't need—"

"He's there."

Brenda's interruption stopped Joe in full stride, and they all turned to look at the bus stands fifty yards across the open square where Mort Norris could be clearly seen talking to a young woman. It might have been innocent, but as they watched, the woman threw her arms around Mort's neck and hugged him. Then, together, they climbed onto the bus.

Sheila gaped, Brenda giggled, and Joe was stunned into momentary silence.

"Mort with a bit on the side?" Brenda chuckled again.

"I don't believe it."

Joe found his voice again. "We're jumping to conclusions. There has to be an innocent explanation."

As they made their way into Freshney Place, Sheila reminded them, "Who was the most vociferous campaigner for Cleethorpes when we were planning this weekend? Mort. Come to think of it, I'm sure it was his idea."

Joe cast his mind back to the meeting, and recalled that it was indeed Mort who suggested and then delivered a passionate appeal for a weekend in Cleethorpes. "Less than a coupla hours on the bus. That's good for me and Alma."

He also recalled Alma's insistence that she asked Mort to suggest the place, and when he told the two women, he concluded with, "What the merry dickens are they playing at?"

At the entrance to the shopping mall, Joe hung back to finish his cigarette, agreeing to contact them when he was ready, and while they disappeared into the increasing crowds, he found a spare bench, sat down and put a fresh light to his smoke. It was one of the irritations with hand-rolled cigarettes that, like cigars, they had a tendency to go out.

Mort Norris with a lover? Mort Norris with a lover in Grimsby of all places? It defied logic, and it defied Alma's earlier declaration.

Joe realised at once that in many cases there was no logic to such liaisons. George Robson was too chubby to be described as a 'hunk' but he enjoyed a reputation for dating the single, divorced, widowed – and sometimes married – women of Sanford. Since his divorce, Joe himself had enjoyed fleeting relationships with a number of women, and he hardly fitted the bill as a lothario. Dating and more intimate affiliations, he knew, had as much to do with personality as appearance.

But Mort Norris?

Thanks to multiple sclerosis, Alma rarely joined him on the 3rd Age Club excursions, but encouraged him to enjoy himself. Their son or daughter would care for Alma while Mort was away. And yet, in all the outings, holidays and so on he had joined, Joe had never seen him so much as look at another woman. To find him hugging, kissing a strange woman in the street, was completely out of character. Had it been in the Sanford area, Joe could have found any number of explanations, but here in Grimsby…

A long lost son or daughter was out of the question. Like so many of the club members, Mort had grown up alongside Joe, and the two children produced by his marriage to Alma were, to Joe's certain knowledge, his only offspring. In fact, Joe knew him well enough to know that he had no links to Humberside, North or South.

And, of course, there was Alma to consider. She and Mort had been married a long time; at least thirty years to Joe's knowledge. How would that poor woman react to learning that her husband was having a long-distance affair? Unless she already knew and had given Mort her blessing, hence her insistence upon Cleethorpes. There were people who, when one partner suffered serious disability like Alma, arranged for 'open' marriage. It was a possibility, and Joe didn't know that side of Mort's marriage well enough to judge one way or the other.

It was with a feeling of confusion tinged with disappointment that he finished his cigarette, and ambled into the shopping mall. He and Alison had been together ten years, and although their marriage foundered, it was not because of infidelity on either side. It was, instead, a marked disparity in their attitude to work and leisure. Joe worked,

Alison preferred time off.

Earlier in the day, when Joe said Freshney Place was similar to Sanford's Galleries Shopping Centre, Brenda hinted that it was ten times the size, and as he dropped onto one of the main thoroughfares through the mall, Joe had to admit she was right. It seemed to him that every well-known familiar name from the high street could be found in that massive, brightly lit, multi-thoroughfare centre, and even at this hour on Saturday (it was not yet eleven o'clock) the place thronged with people. Finding Sheila and Brenda would be a work of art.

Instead, he stepped into a coffee shop, ordered a cup of tea and took a table near the door. Once settled, he dipped into one of the multitude of pockets in his gilet, retrieved a notebook and pen, and opening it at a fresh page, began to list the possible reasons for Mort meeting a woman.

By the time he had finished, it did not make pleasant reading. A clandestine affair was top of the list, and beneath it the various other excuses e.g. distant relative, distant friend, former colleague, made little sense when ranged alongside the history of a man who to Joe's knowledge has never strayed further from Sanford than Leeds, and only then to visit wholesalers. Colleagues were a nonstarter. Relying on his memory once again, Joe recalled that after a brief spell of employment in a warehouse when he left school Mort had worked for himself most of his life.

Twenty minutes later, his phone rang. Brenda looking for him. He told them where to find him, and a few minutes after that, they joined him. They had been in the shopping mall less than half an hour, and already they were laden with bags full of purchases.

Over a cup of tea, Sheila studied his list of headings, and came to the reluctant conclusion that he was right.

Brenda found it funny. "Mort Norris. Who'd have thought it?"

Joe frowned upon her humour. "I was thinking of poor Alma. If she doesn't already know, what will it do to her if she finds out?"

"Well, we're not going to tell her, are we?" Sheila objected.

"True, but what about the rest of the gang? You know what the Sanford 3rd Age Club is like. One rumour of Mort meeting another woman, and by the time they spread the news, he'll have an entire harem all over the north of England."

"In that case, Joe, someone will have to have a word with Mort."

Sheila's statement oozed meaning, and combined with a steadfast gaze, Joe knew that the 'someone' would be him.

Brenda encouraged him. "Mano-a-Mano, Joe."

He frowned again. "For your information, Mano-a-Mano means hand to hand, not man-to-man. And what the hell will I say to him? Listen, Mort, it's not cricket, you floating off with your bit on the side while your kids are looking after Alma."

Brenda pouted. "Hmm. It needs work, Joe. A little more polish."

"It doesn't matter how much glitter I put on it, you know what he'll say. Sod off and mind your own business. Nah, if you're looking for someone to give Mort fatherly advice, try Norman Pyecock."

"Norman? He'd probably applaud Mort." Brenda tutted. "Why do you men have such a problem keeping your pants on?"

"Hark at who's talking. You're…"

Joe trailed off as Sheila guided him with urgent flashes of her eyes, looking to him, insisting that he follow her gaze beyond the café. He half turned in time to see two men walking hand in hand towards them.

Joe clucked. "Do they have to be so brazen about it?"

"No. Joe—"

Brenda cut Sheila off. "You've never been homophobic, Joe."

"I'm not. But that's not the point. Do they have to walk through a busy shopping centre holding hands?"

Sheila tried to butt in yet again, but Brenda carried on

speaking over her. "Do you have any problem with a man and woman holding hands? No. You have any problem with a couple of women holding hands? No. So what's the difference if it's two men? Love is love, Joe, and you find it wherever you can, and when you do, you let the world know about it."

"I'm not arguing about that. I'm simply saying… Oh, all right, all right. So I'm old-fashioned."

"Good. As long as that's all it is." Brenda's face expressed satisfaction. "We've never been guilty of racism, sexism, or any kind of ism, have we?"

Sheila's face registered impatience. "Well here's an example of bad temper-ism. While you were debating the rights and wrongs of gay men holding hands in public, you missed something about the men in question which was far more important."

Joe raised his eyebrows. "Such as?"

"They were both members of the Shoreline Swingsters."

# Chapter Nine

Joe continued to chew his thoughts throughout the rest of the morning and into the afternoon. Sex and money, Sergeant Watney had said. The biggest motives for murder, and both were possibilities in the killing of Paul Caswell. But how to isolate *the* motive?

From Freshney Place, they made their way through the streets of Grimsby taking in Freeman Street market, an indoor hall which looked no better than a warehouse from the outside, but once indoors was as refreshingly modern as any other outlet in the town.

After a light lunch at a restaurant close to the docks, they paid a visit to the Fishing Heritage Centre, and spent an hour wandering the exhibits before visiting the souvenir shop, where Joe bought a model trawler and then wondered where it might display in The Lazy Luncheonette.

"You'll have to put a new shelf up," Sheila said.

"And high up," Brenda advised. "Some of those draymen are way too tall, and we don't want them getting caught in its nets, do we?"

Afterwards they moved further along the docks so Joe could take a range of photographs of the spectacular Grimsby Dock Tower, a stark, three-hundred-plus foot edifice modelled on the Torre del Mangia in Siena. It was a landmark clearly visible on most approaches to the town, and he recalled that it had been a marker on the way back from Rotterdam some years previously. Those distant views paled alongside the close up sight. It was at once magnificent and domineering, and Joe could imagine the relief the fishermen of yesteryear experienced when they first caught sight of it on the inbound journey.

By half past two, they were beginning to tire, and they caught the bus for the fifteen minute journey back to Cleethorpes.

From Joe's point of view it had been a satisfying yet confusing day. His mind churned with the possibilities and probabilities behind the murder of Paul Caswell. It called to mind the cases he had investigated in York, Weston-super-Mare, and Whitby; cases where none of his members were implicated, but which had occurred on the periphery of their visits and he had shoved his oar in to help the police. It was precisely the action the present conundrum called for.

And thrown into the mix were the guilt-saturated, inexplicable actions of Mort Norris, the last man anyone would suspect of clandestine behaviour.

It made for a complex weekend, with no easy solution on the horizon.

The heat of the bright afternoon sunshine magnified by the bus windows, caused him to remove his topcoat, but the moment they got off the bus, that chilly wind enveloped him, and he put it back on for the quarter-mile walk to the Queen Elizabeth.

Laden with bags of various shapes and sizes, Joe stumbling and grumbling along with a huge bag containing his model trawler, when they entered the hotel his first port of call was reception where Turgot greeted him with a disdainful eye.

Joe ignored it. "Can you tell me whether Mort Norris has been back to the hotel since we first arrived?"

"It is not this hotel's policy to keep a track on its guests, Mr Murray. It would be an unforgivable invasion of privacy."

"I'm not asking for a detailed record of his comings and goings. I just want to know if you've seen him."

"If I had I wouldn't recognise him, and if I had I still would not tell you. As I said, it would be an invasion—"

"Of privacy. I know." Joe scowled. "You know that sign outside, the one that says 'welcome'? Did you put it up for a joke?"

He didn't wait for an answer, but walked away making for

the lift and his third floor room.

Once inside, he was relieved to be rid of the model trawler, which he stowed in the wardrobe. As he stripped off his outer clothing, he questioned the sanity of buying such a bulky item. It would make more sense to order it online and pay for delivery.

He was about to switch the kettle on when there was a knock at the door. Opening it, he found Sheila who greeted him with a smile. "We're about to have a quick cuppa. Fancy joining us? We have a wonderful sea view."

"That's the best invitation I've had all day."

He picked up his keys, stepped out of the room, and making sure the door was locked, crossed the corridor to theirs, but before he could step in, he noticed one of the housekeepers leaving a room further along the corridor.

"Be with you in a minute, Sheila." He hurried along the corridor to catch up with the housekeeper who was examining her skirt, tutting and fussing as she brushed it down.

"Excuse me."

She stopped what she was doing, looked up and smiled. "Yes, sir?"

"Muck and dust, huh?" he pointed to her skirt.

"You'd never believe how grubby this job can be. And if Mr Turgot spots anything out of place, he goes off on one. And they only give you the one uniform, you know, and you have to clean and press it yourself."

"Employers, eh? Who'd have 'em? And your boss needs a lesson in staff motivation. Refer him to me if he's in any doubt."

"Anyway, what can I do for you, sir?"

"Well, you can stop calling me sir for a start off. I'm not an officer and I'm certainly not a gentleman. I'm Joe Murray, but you can call me Joe."

"I couldn't do that, sir. Mr Turgot would hit the roof if he heard me."

"Yes, but he's not here. Listen…" Joe checked her nametag to ensure it was the same girl who had spilled the drinks tray the previous evening. "Vicky, do you know if you're looking after Mr and Mrs Norris's room? They're with our party; the Sanford 3rd Age Club."

"I think so, sir. The lady in the wheelchair."

"The very woman. Could you tell me whether Mort, her husband, has been back to the hotel since we arrived?"

Vicky blushed. "I couldn't say, sir. I'm not allowed."

Joe sighed and made a conscious effort to control his irritation. "Listen, luv, turbo-man isn't here, and I'm not going to tell him, but we're a little concerned about Mr Norris. Please, help us out."

She hesitated yet again. "I really can't say, sir, but I can tell you this. Only one of the beds in that room has been slept in, and I believe it's Mrs Norris's."

"Thank you. You're an angel." Joe tapped the side of his nose. "But not a word to the turbocharger, eh?"

She giggled, turned and went on her way, and Joe returned to the women's room.

He was immediately impressed by the amount of space they had, and further irritated at the space he did not have. His annoyance was compounded by the spectacular view of the Humber Estuary from the table stood by the single window. The sun continued to blaze from a cloudless sky, and in the distance, beyond the ships passing one way or another, he could see the tiny spike of Spurn Head Lighthouse. Closer to home, Ross Castle, a folly built on the edge of Pier Gardens stood like a small sentry watching over the coastline. He could see beyond Pier Gardens to the promenade where people ambled along in both directions, wrapped up against the cold breeze but savouring the sunshine and the fresh, sea air.

Brenda served tea, Sheila laid out biscuits, and when they were settled, they honed their concentration on Joe.

"News?" Sheila demanded.

"All negative. I just spoke to that maid, Vicky—"

"I believe they're called housekeepers these days, Joe."

"Don't confuse the issue, Brenda. I couldn't care less if they're known as accommodation hygiene technicians. We know who I'm talking about. Anyway, she told me that Mort is still officially AWOL."

It was not what they wanted to hear as was evident from their downcast faces.

"I don't know what's going on, but I can't help thinking about Alma. If Mort's playing away from home, who's going to break the news to her?" Joe took a sip of tea. "And don't look at me. I'm not telling her."

Brenda looked away and it was left to Sheila to bring a sense of moderation to the debate. "I think we're jumping the gun. Like you said, we're making assumptions and we could be totally off the mark. It's not Alma we need to worry about, Joe, it's Mort. As we said earlier, someone needs to speak to him, and that's better coming from you."

"Can we talk about something else?" Brenda asked. "Something less delicate? Like, what are the Shoreline Swingsters going to do without a trombonist?"

"Get Norman Pyecock up playing the spoons?" Joe's silly remark was intended to follow Brenda's lead and lighten the mood. "Or maybe we can get George Robson up to give us a rousing chorus of Nessun Dorma."

Brenda laughed. "No go. George probably thinks Nessun Dorma is a Japanese campervan. And have you heard him sing? The last time he picked up the karaoke mike in the Miners Arms, every dog in Sanford was howling in sympathy."

Joe helped himself to a Rich Tea biscuit, bit into it, and swallowed it with a mouthful of tea. "You do have a point, though, Brenda. What I know about musical arrangement, you could write on a Post-It note and still leave room for a best man's speech, but whoever their arranger is, he'll have his work cut out to be ready by tonight."

"Probably the bandleader. Tommy, what's his name? Loudmouth."

"Louden," Sheila corrected her, "as you well know."

"Which reminds me, I need a quiet word with him about his missus."

Shock registered on both women's faces.

Brenda recovered first. "What? You're going to poke your nose into her affairs by asking her husband? And for once I'm using word affairs literally. It's probably the quickest way to a broken nose."

"Credit me with some tact."

Sheila chuckled. "I think you ran out of credit in that department a long time ago."

"I don't have to sit here to listen to these insults, you know. I can go anywhere." He drank his tea and yawned. "Five o'clock. Time I was getting some shut eye. I'll catch you both later, in the dining room."

He left the room, fully intending to return to his and taking a nap, but the nicotine craving overtook him, and instead, he made his way downstairs and out to the front of the hotel where he found Tommy Louden staring glumly from the bench out across Pier Gardens to the sea beyond.

"All right, sport?" Joe asked as he took a seat at the opposite end of the bench and began to roll a cigarette.

"I've had better weekends." The accent was a thick, West Midlands, a contrast to his classless English when performing the previous evening. "What about you? Enjoying your break?"

Joe shivered convincingly. "It's a change. Could do with being a bit warmer, mind."

"You should've been here in January. You'd know what cold means."

Having set up a cigarette, Joe put it between his lips and lit up. Blowing out smoke with an audible hiss, he recalled Rose mentioning a visit at the start of the year. "I thought yesterday was your opening set."

"It was, but me and Rose and Paul Caswell came here early in the year to suss the place out. We stayed in this dump for three nights, finding digs for the band, working on the ballroom layout so we could set up properly. We were working a dance hall in Birmingham at the time, and it was a rotten journey both ways. Bloody cold, mate. But we got organised and that's what matters."

Joe changed the subject. "And talking of Paul Caswell, we

were all sorry to hear about him."

Louden grunted. "That's what I meant when I said I've had better weekends."

"I was just talking to my friends about it. What do you do in that situation? Drag in another trombonist?"

The bandleader laughed, but there was no humour in it. "In Cleethorpes? At such short notice? Nah. You couldn't get another slidy sam in and bring him up to snuff in so short a time. No, mate, we have to rearrange the pieces, cut Paul out, cover with other instruments."

"Lotta work for you, I suppose."

"We could do without it."

Joe puffed on his cigarette. "Tell you what, we were talking between ourselves earlier, and we were trying to figure out how you guys work it. I mean, judging by your accent, you're obviously not from round here, yet you're booked for the season. Surely you don't commute every day."

"From Brum? Do we hell as like. I said, didn't I, we were here organising digs for the band. Me and the missus, Rosie – you saw her last night. She's the main vocalist. Well, me and her, we've rented a house in Grimsby, from now until September. Paul was in digs somewhere in Cleethorpes. Big Cam, the horn player, he's in digs somewhere near here, too, Heather and Nige Hollis, she's keyboards, he's alto sax, they've taken a caravan on a park near here. Ed and Billy – bass and skins – they're an item so they're sharing a bed in the same digs as Paul, and they leave their gear here. Diane's somewhere local and so is Freddie, the second trumpet." He chuckled. "We're a motley mob, but we've been together for, oh, five years now, give or take."

"You'll be here next season, huh?"

The big man shrugged. "Could be, but Accomplus, the company as what owns this gig, might ask us to move to… I dunno… Blackpool, Skeggy, even Brighton or Bournemouth. No offence, mate, but our kinda music appeals to oldies like you, and we go wherever they're expected."

Joe's laugh was as false as Louden's. "No sale. A lot of my members like your stuff, but personally, I'd rather have

Abba."

"Especially the blonde?"

"Especially the blonde."

Joe made a point of checking his watch, and then crushed out his cigarette. "Well, time I was getting some shuteye. I'll catch... you are on tonight, are you?"

"Showbiz tradition, mate. The show must go on. First set's supposed to be eight, but it might be later."

"Catch you later, then."

Joe returned to his room, the confusion of events slightly cleared. There was a long way to go, but Tommy's information, allied to the sight of Rose Louden and Paul Caswell making their way into Sunbeams B&B, and her admission first thing that morning, was complicated by the knowledge that two other band members were in the same lodging house.

Was it, he asked himself, a cue for blackmail which then led to murder? It was virtually the last thought on his mind before he drifted into a much-needed nap.

\*\*\*

"How well do you know Alma?" Brenda asked as she sat before the dresser applying makeup.

Trying to decide between a colourfully decorated, loose-fitting top and more sombre, navy blue blouse, Sheila considered the question. "Not well. She's not a Sanforder. I think she comes from Wakefield originally. Mort met her through a lonely hearts ad when he was in his mid- twenties." Opting for the plain blouse, she sat on the edge of the bed while fastening the buttons. "We've known Mort since school. Working on his market stall, he could sell you a meat pie and swear it was vegetarian, but when it came to women, he was a bit like Joe; clumsy, out of his depth. But when you speak to Alma—"

"Which aside from club do's is not very often," Brenda interrupted.

"Granted, but when you do, she insists he's a model

husband. That goes double now she's virtually confined to the wheelchair. She relies upon Mort for almost everything and Lord knows what will happen to her if he decides he's had enough." Sheila sighed. "It's what makes this business so puzzling."

"Still waters," Brenda said. "Didn't someone say it's always the quiet ones?"

"I think it might have been you, dear."

Brenda laughed. "Yeah. Probably." Wearing only a bra and underskirt, she turned from the mirror to face her best friend. "But we're jumping to conclusions, aren't we?"

"Can you think of an innocent explanation for what we saw at the bus stop?"

This time, it was Brenda who gave the question consideration before reluctantly shaking her head. "No. No I can't. I mean, neither of their kids live or work in this area, do they?"

"I think Mort junior works for Broadbent's opposite The Lazy Luncheonette, and Rebecca worked at the Town Hall… Sanford Town Hall, I mean, not Grimsby. And I think they're both married and settled in Sanford."

"And I'm sure he said they look out for Alma when he's away with the 3rd Age Club and she isn't." Brenda shrugged and turned back to the mirror. "They have no other kids, and that woman looked too young to be a sister or anything, so who the hell was she?"

"Do you know what worries me, Brenda?" Sheila did not wait for a response. "Joe. You know what he's like when he gets the bit between his teeth. He's like a Rottweiler. He won't let go. It wouldn't take much to alienate Mort to the point of…well, I don't know. Violence, I suppose."

Brenda laughed again, more sarcastically this time. "If you wrapped Joe in tissue paper and told him to fight his way out of it, the tissue paper would win. Crikey, we used to protect him at school, didn't we? Us, George, Owen, Alec. Joe might have been the gang leader, but we were the foot soldiers. And Mort is the same. He was never a scrapper."

Sheila tutted. "I didn't necessarily mean physical violence.

I meant verbal. Joe will have his say, and Mort will retaliate. We're all friends, Brenda. Despite the odd fall out, like you and him in Cornwall, for instance, or that business with Martin the other Christmas, the 3rd Age Club runs on friendship, doesn't it? That kind of animosity we can do without." She chewed her lip. "But how do we get Joe to learn the language of diplomacy?"

Brenda almost collapsed in fits of laughter.

"What's so funny?"

"I was thinking of the time old Ned Spurling died. He ran the chippy on Leeds Road, right next door to where Cyril Peck lived, and they were big mates, Ned and Cyril. Someone delegated Joe to break the news, and told him to break it gently on account of how Cyril and Ned were bosom buddies. And what did Joe say? I've some bad news for you, Cyril; you'll have to walk a bit further for your fish and chips in future."

Sheila giggled. "Typical Joe. How would he put this business to Mort?"

Brenda pondered the proposition. "Something like; hey up, Mort, is it true your Alma's running another lonely hearts ad?"

They enjoyed another good laugh.

Sheila sobered first. "Seriously though, I'm wondering if it's wise asking Joe to handle the matter."

"No, it isn't, but let's be honest, neither you nor I could handle it, could we? I know your attitude to infidelity, Sheila, and no matter what my reputation as a merry widow, you know mine. In all the years Colin and I were married, I never once betrayed him. Blunt as Joe might be, I think you and I would be a lot harder on Mort... Assuming we have it right, that is."

"And if we don't?"

"Then leave it to Joe. He has a higher threshold of embarrassment. He can take it when he's wrong." Finished with make-up, Brenda got to her feet and opened the wardrobe door. "That's the war paint on. All I need now is the battle gear."

## Chapter Ten

At half past five, with the sun dipping towards the horizon somewhere behind the hotel, Joe was outside, enjoying another smoke while telling himself he really needed to stop again, when George Robson and Owen Frickley returned from wherever their afternoon adventures had taken them.

They were the same age as Joe, and like him, both were divorced. Unlike him, they tended to make the most of life, but then, neither man was self-employed. George was a foreman gardener for Sanford Borough Council, Owen, also a charge-hand, was what could be termed a general maintenance operative, a job which was impossible to define, but involved cleaning up the housing estates in and around the town. The contrast between the three men was striking. Where Joe was small, wiry, quick on his feet if not over-endowed with physical strength, George was big, beefy, bulky, and noticeably overweight. Owen was taller than George, square shouldered, muscular, and unlike his drinking pal, kept himself in fairly good shape.

They were serious drinkers without suffering an addiction to alcohol, but their voluminous intake of beer had often led to arguments and outright fights especially on those occasions when George, also a notorious womaniser, made an effort to 'pull' some woman who was attached to another party.

Despite their slightly bohemian lifestyle, both men remained philosophical.

"It's what life's all about," George would often say. "Getting tanked up, getting your end away, and getting into the odd ruck." By and large, Owen agreed with him, but as they climbed out of the taxi and walked unsteadily towards the hotel, they were obviously arguing about something.

Joe was pleased to see it. It distracted his mind from the murder of Paul Caswell and Mort Norris's curious behaviour.

"You let your mouth run away with you," Owen was saying as they neared the entrance.

Without knowing what had happened, Joe could nevertheless draw the scenario in his head. They had been in a pub, George tried it on with some woman, whose husband/partner/significant other took offence, and from there matters went downhill with a speed far in excess of anything Joe could manage when dealing with the Sanford Brewery's draymen demanding breakfast.

With a sense of self-indulgent pleasure, he realised the accuracy of his guess when they drew near enough for him to spot a bruise on George's cheek. He chuckled to himself, took another drag on his cigarette, and after the customary coughing fit, greeted them.

"World War Ten?"

Owen sniffed and jerked a thumb sideways at George. "Big mouth, here. Bit off more than he could chew for once."

"Well I didn't know, did I?"

Joe patted a space on the bench alongside him. "Sit down and tell me all about it."

They took up the remaining seats, George dabbing a handkerchief against his bruised cheek, Owen digging into his pocket for a pack of cigarettes.

"Were the cops involved?" Joe asked.

Owen lit up and blew smoke into the clear air. "Nope. We weren't in a pub, anyway. It was outside that shopping centre in Grimsby."

"We've been there most of the day. I never saw you."

"No, but we saw you and ducked out of the way."

Joe ignored George's sneer. "Go on then, Owen. Tell me the worst."

"We bumped into the gay boys in the band. Billy wossname and Ed foxtrot."

"Foxton," Joe corrected.

"Whoever. Course, gobby here had to open his trap, didn't

he? Called them a couple of poofters, and they heard him. They complained that he was being politically incorrect, and it could be hate speech." Owen took another drag on his cigarette. "Well, you know the mouth, here. Wouldn't shut it, would he? We followed them and George was arguing the toss about them holding hands in public, they were telling him to mind his own bloody business, he threatened them, and that Billy, he told tubby here to give it his best shot. That's like a red rag to a bull where George is concerned. He threw a punch, and Billy boy kicked him on the cheek."

Joe was surprised. George stood about five feet nine, and he was puzzled as to how someone could kick him on the cheek. "So was George laid out or something?"

"He was after Billy the kicker booted him."

"I don't understand. Was Billy standing on a chair? How did he manage to kick him on the jaw?"

Owen laughed and took yet another drag on his cigarette. "No. Turns out he has a black belt in take one dough."

"You mean taekwondo."

"I knew it was something from Japan."

"Korea, if I'm not mistaken," Joe said.

"Stop nitpicking," George said. "They're all the same, aren't they? Bloody little—"

Owen interrupted. "Shut your fat gob, George. It's caused enough trouble for one lifetime." He concentrated on Joe. "Have you seen anything of Mort?"

"We spotted him in Grimsby. You?"

Owen licked his lips and when he spoke it was with burning enthusiasm. "Have we ever. After this tosser was done hassling with Grimsby's Bruce Lee lookalike, we had a couple of beers, and as we came out of this pub, we saw Mort getting off a bus, and you should have seen the bint he was with. Tell you what, Joe, I wouldn't mind climbing over you to get to her. Classy? Huge boobydoos trapped in a tight T-shirt, short skirt, legs all the way up to her—"

"I get the picture, Owen." Joe chewed his lip. "What the hell is he playing at?"

The first time since they arrived, George chuckled.

"Showjumping… Well, jumping, and this time it's an away match."

"And he has to be paying for it, Joe," Owen ventured. "I mean, no way would a woman like that look twice at an old scroat like Mort."

"You're jumping to conclusions, both of you. But if it's right, someone has to have a word with him, and Sheila and Brenda are trying to lay the job on me."

"Want me to deal with him?" George asked. "If he gives me an introduction to this tart, I'll advise him of the dangers involved in playing away from home."

"And what about Alma?"

George shook his head and winced as the pain in his cheek bit again. "I don't fancy Alma."

Joe fumed. "I meant what will it do to her, you berk. Hell's bells, she practically relies on Mort for everything. What is the bloody fool trying to do?"

"You could always mind your own business, Joe," Owen suggested.

"That'd be a first," George said.

"Bog off, you." Joe concentrated on Owen. "I'm trying to mind my own business, but Mavis Barker and Cyril Peck keep hassling me, Sheila and Brenda are giving me earache, but when I spoke to Alma this morning, she all but told me to mind my own bloody business."

George spread his large hands. "That's it then. If Alma knows and she doesn't care, why are you bothering? Maybe you're in with a chance, Joe. I mean, you might need a lift onto the bed, but—"

Once again, Joe interrupted. "If you don't shut it, George, I'll…" A physical assault out of the question, he racked his mind for some suitable threat. "I'll make you stand me three pints tonight."

Owen finished his cigarette, crushed it out on the stubber, and dropped the remains in a large ashtray attached to the hotel wall. "Sitting here, chatting about Mort Norris won't get me fed and watered. What's the crack here, tonight, Joe? Not that band again? What with one of them topped last night."

"I was speaking to Tommy Louden earlier, and he insists they're playing tonight."

George grunted. "That's it, then. What say we hit the town, Owen?"

"Sounds good to me. We'll catch you later, Joe."

Joe checked his watch and learned that it was almost quarter to six. Time he was getting back to the room and changing for dinner and the night's entertainment.

"Better have another smoke first," he muttered to himself as a small, dark-coloured van pulled into the car park and stopped.

Lighting yet another cigarette, he watched with interest as Campbell Arnholt climbed out of the rear and with an audible, "Thanks, guys," hurried along the side of the hotel. The front doors opened and Billy Warner and Ed Foxton climbed out, Foxton locked the vehicle, and they too made for the side of the hotel, and – so Joe assumed – the 'tradesmen's entrance' Turgot was so insistent the band used.

They were dressed in what Joe assumed was the official band uniform: royal blue blazer, grey pants, white shirt and ties with the Shoreline Swingsters logo printed on them, but he noticed they also sported black armbands on their right sleeves. Respect for Paul Caswell.

Joe called to them. "Spare me a minute or two, guys."

They turned in his direction, and smiles spread across their faces.

"Oh, Billy, the detective wants a word with us."

"Cost you a fiver for a few minutes with me, luv," Warner chuckled.

"All right, all right, you can cut the camp act. Until I saw you in Freshney Place earlier today I had no idea you were an item, so you can stick to your normal macho behaviour."

They ranged themselves alongside him, and Foxton went onto the attack. "Are our living arrangements anything to do with you?"

"No, but—"

"When you're at a dinner party do you introduce yourself as, 'Hello, I'm Joe Murray and I'm straight'?"

"Well, no, but—"

"There you are then. We are a gay couple. We're not ashamed of that, but it's not something we announce as a matter of routine."

"Right. It's nothing to do with anyone, including me, but lamping one of my members is, and—"

Warner interrupted. "You mean that ignorant lout who badmouthed and threatened us?"

"George Robson."

"Yes, well, George Robson threw the first punch," Warner said. "I merely defended us."

Joe sighed. "If you shut up long enough to listen, I was going to apologise for his behaviour on behalf of the Sanford 3rd Age Club."

"Ah."

"Oh."

Joe puffed on his cigarette and took a few moments to compose his thoughts. He was concerned more with the murder of Paul Caswell than the incident between this pair and George Robson, but that same altercation gave him a nice lead into it.

"You have to forgive George. Like the rest of us, he comes from a rough, tough mining area, and we're all a bit old-fashioned."

"You don't have gay men in Sanford?"

"Of course we do, and of course they're entitled to their lifestyle, and of course the vast majority of us accept that. Unfortunately, George isn't one of them. His wife left him for another woman."

It was an out and out lie. George's wife left him because of his habit of jumping into bed with other women, but even though Joe considered George's actions with this pair to be thoroughly reprehensible and unforgivable, he felt it might help smooth waters with Foxton and Warner.

He was wrong, as Foxton was quick to point out. "Regardless of that, there was no excuse for his behaviour. How would you like it, Mr Murray, if I described you as a breeder?"

"I'd say you were wrong."

Joe's response took both men aback. Warner recovered first. "Oh, so you are—"

"No, I am not gay, but I'm not a breeder either. During the ten years I was married, my wife and I had no children."

Foxton wagged a disapproving finger at him. "Don't get technical. You know what I mean."

"Yes I do, and George's behaviour was beyond the pale. As I said, accept my apology on behalf of the Sanford 3rd Age Club." He drew on his cigarette again, suffered a short but violent coughing fit, coupled to a violent stab of pain in his upper left chest and a twinge in his left arm. Slightly alarmed, he went on. "Do any members of the band object to you?"

"They wouldn't dare."

When Joe frowned, both men laughed, and Foxton launched into the story. "We know too much about them, you see. Whisper has it that you've already rumbled the naughty business between Rose and Paul Caswell. Everyone knows about it, including Tommy, but he never complains about it because while Rose and Paul were up to their shenanigans, Tommy was busy tumbling with Diane, the sax player. She daren't open her mouth because when she's not horizontal with Tommy, she is doing the business with Nigel Hollis, and she has history with Caswell. Nigel can't say anything about anything because he's married to Heather, who is getting her jollies with Freddie Brackley, and she, too, had more than one interlude with Caswell."

Joe struggled to sort the information. "Was Caswell going for a world record, or something?"

"Rumour has it that he was partying with a member of staff here in January when he and Tommy came to look the place over. Foot lose and fancy free, our Mr Caswell."

"But according to Tommy, Rose was with them on that trip."

"True, but Paul could hardly jump on Rose while Tommy was sleeping alongside her, could he?"

"No. I suppose not."

Warner took over. "When I think about it, Mr Murray, the only people in a serious, monogamous relationship are Ed and myself. We don't see other people, we don't sleep with anyone else."

Joe spent a moment trying to make headway through the bewildering information, and at length asked, "What about Campbell Arnholt? It seems to me that you've run out of women, so who's he sleeping with?"

"His bookie, I shouldn't wonder. He certainly owes the man enough money, and from what we've seen, the bookie's wife is a good deal younger, so maybe Cam's paying in kind."

The remark reminded Joe of the argument he'd witnessed the previous day between Caswell and Arnholt. "Another whisper is that Arnholt is short of money."

"No big secret," Foxton said. "He's always broke. Why do you think he scrounges a lift from us? We're in the same digs, and he has no car. It was repossessed. Between his ex-wife's demands for child support, and his bookie's demands to pay up, Cam is what's known as brassic, peppermint, skint, not living next door to flat broke, but actually living with flat broke."

Warner concurred. "The way things are going, I'll be very surprised if Cam is with us next year. In fact, I'll be very surprised if he sees this season out. He can't afford it." He focused a narrow stare on Joe. "You're the little tell-tale, aren't you? The man who'll go running to the police with every tiny bit of tittle tattle?"

Joe had had enough of the goading. "Listen to me, sunshine. I've investigated more murders than you've attended gay conventions. I've help the police put killers behind bars all over the country. I'll tell Karen Gipton everything I learn, true, and somewhere along the line, I guarantee that I will pin down the person who tried to kill Rose Louden and killed Caswell by mistake."

The announcement took them both by surprise. Foxton was the first to recover. "Rose?"

"I spoke to her this morning. When you people were

sorting the drinks out last night, Caswell picked up her spritzer, and she got his Tom Collins. The poison that killed Caswell was meant for her. Now you're the gossip merchants, you tell me, who in the band would want rid of Rose Louden?"

He expected them to fall quiet, but they did not. The speed with which Warner answered, told him that they needed no time in coming to a conclusion.

"Heather Hollis."

Joe's eyebrows rose. "She's keyboards, isn't she?"

"And second vocalist. Get rid of Rose, and she's the only singer in the band... Correction. She's the only singer in the band as it is."

"Better than Rose?"

Foxton nodded. "Streets ahead of her, but, of course, she can't get a look in. Rose is Tommy's wife. Nuff said. And, think about this. If Rose wasn't lead vocalist, what else would she do? Play the bloody tambourine? Pah. Anyone can tap a handheld drum."

"She doesn't play any instruments, then?"

"All she can play is the merry hell."

The two men left, Joe finished his cigarette, endured another coughing fit, and returned to his room.

Half an hour later, he settled into his seat at the dining table, and while he studied the menu, he related the tale to Sheila and Brenda.

Concentrating finally on Brenda, he said, "You know you said they were called Swingsters because of the naughty connotations of the word 'swingers'? The way those two boys told me the tale, I think I had it right in the first place. They do so much bed-hopping, they should be the Shoreline Swingers."

Brenda grinned. "Ooh. I wonder if they have a vacancy?"

Sheila chuckled along. "Can you play the trombone?"

"No, but you should see me slide between the sheets."

# Chapter Eleven

With the time coming up to half past seven, dinner over, Sheila and Brenda made their way to the ballroom while Joe, promising to catch up with them before the Shoreline Swingsters were due onstage, slipped into the lounge bar. Aside from when they were busy filling out the check-in forms, it was the first time he had stepped across the threshold, and he was not surprised to find it almost empty. Most of the patrons, and indeed the non-residents, would make for the ballroom and the evening's entertainment.

It was not a large room; not when compared to, say, the Palmer Hotel, another Accomplus site about ten miles out of York, which was run by his friend Yvonne Vallance. What the Queen Elizabeth lacked in style it tried to make up for in grandeur... or at least, the Accomplus group's idea of grandeur. A lot of oak panelling and beams, a bar decked with the trite brasses so familiar in a seaside town, and walls covered in flock wallpaper and liberally situated, framed photographs of Cleethorpes old and new, the Queen Elizabeth old and new.

To his relief, Turgot was not serving. Probably taking a break before getting behind the bar in the ballroom, but Joe made a mental note to speak with the manager at some point. It would, he knew, be one of the more awkward face-to-face question and answer sessions and he wanted to speak to Yvonne first.

For now, he had other members of the Shoreline Swingsters to deal with and he guessed it would not be plain sailing.

George and Owen were propping up the bar, talking to Campbell Arnholt, but aside from them and a few other individuals, none of whom Joe recognised, the band were the only people in the bar, and they were spread about the room in different, small cliques. Tommy and Freddie Brackley, billed as second trumpet, were in one corner, deep in conversation, sheet music spread across the table hinted that they were discussing the new arrangements. No doubt Tommy wanted Freddie to take on some of Caswell's parts.

Composing and arranging music on an orchestral level, or even for a band as small as this, was a skill Joe admired, if only from a distance. He could write. At one point, he had made a point of writing up his cases and had them privately printed for the customers in the old Lazy Luncheonette, before it burned down. Nowadays, he did not bother, but he still summarised them on his laptop. They were useful as reminders of the awful events he had come across, and they were in place against the day when he might be called to court as a witness.

Music, however, was a different and much tougher proposition. He had never been musically inclined. He bought a cheap guitar when he was in his teens, but he never mastered anything other than the basic chords and when it came to melody, he never progressed any further than Camptown Races.

Lyrics, he surmised, would be the easier task. It was poetry (another skill in which he was never better than basic). But where did the melody come from? And once that was sorted, how did the composer decide on the key? When all that was done, how did a man like Louden fit it into the various instruments of his band, how did he decide which instrument should pick up which part? At the side of that, rustling up lamb cutlets in red wine followed by upside down pudding, both of which he had enjoyed at dinner, was child's play.

Further round, Billy Warner and Ed Foxton sat alone, chatting, a few seats away Heather Hollis and her husband, Nigel, sat in silence, and from the look of thunder on their faces, Joe would bet it was a domestic disagreement. Heather's eye occasionally strayed towards Rose Louden, who sat with Diane Stott, and the glares reminded Joe of Warner and Foxton's opinion on the one most likely to want Rose out of the way.

And as for that final pair… it was obvious that Rose and Diane were involved in a heated argument. Joe could not hear what they were saying, and the speed at which Rose's mouth moved would defy any lip-reader. She emphasised her point by jabbing a bony finger into the table top. Not to be outdone, Diane fought back with the same, sibilant volume, but with a determination which belied her slight build and appearance, and which refused to buckle under to Rose's anger.

With echoes of Warner and Foxton ringing through his head, Joe needed no guesses to work out what they were arguing about. Caswell had slept with both women, and with Heather Hollis, and if the gay couple were to be believed, Tommy had also slept with Diane, and so had Nigel Hollis. Excluding Warner, Foxton, and Arnholt, the band formed a sort of *ménage à sept*. Good fun, Joe assumed, burying his personal disgust for the proposition. Had these people never heard of monogamy?

At some point, he would have to speak to these people individually, but now was not the time. Not while they were wading through internal battles.

He made for the bar and ordered a small beer.

"So, Mr meddlesome, eh?"

It was Arnholt, turning away from George and Owen to smile at Joe.

"You should be careful." Joe nodded to his two friends. "They're members of my party, my gang, and if I can't tackle someone your size, they will."

Arnholt laughed. "What? After Wilhelmina's already kicked his teeth in?" He gestured first at George, then at Warner and Foxton.

Joe remained unimpressed. "Wilhelmina? You're as homophobic as George."

"I am not homophonic, Joe," George complained. "I just don't like 'em, that's all."

"It's the same thing, you daft prat. And it's time you grew up." Handing over the cash for his beer, Joe swung his attention on Arnholt. "The same goes for you. The trouble with hard men like you is that somewhere along the line, they meet their match, and in your case, you're looking at him. I might not be able to flatten you, but I can tie you in so many logical knots that you won't know your knuckles from your kneecaps, and when I've done that, I'll hand you over to the cops as the man who most likely shuffled Caswell off his mortal coil."

Arnholt bristled and Owen came in on Joe's side. "You should listen to him, Cam. We've seen him do it a score of times, and he's a right pain, you know. He won't go away."

The big man scowled down. "Well, you listen to me, Hercules Porridge. I had nothing to do with Caswell's death. Got it?"

"I hear you. That doesn't mean I believe you. I heard that barney between him and you on the seafront on Friday."

Arnholt's scowl became a frown. "What barney?"

"You were telling him you knew where he could stick the slide off his trombone."

Arnholt picked up what looked like a glass of lager but could have been shandy and took a long swallow. "I don't know what you're talking about."

"I heard it. We all did. Me, Sheila and Brenda. You're short of money, and one of the cops investigating this business pointed out that in most cases, the biggest motives for murder are sex and money; and sometimes, it's both."

"Well, in this case, smartarse, you're wrong on both counts. My financial affairs are no business of yours, and I did not kill Caswell. You want a motive, try looking at sex." Once again he waved an arm around the room. "He's had every woman in here, and more besides, and if they didn't get shot of him, try their husbands. For now, get off my back."

He slammed his empty glass on the bar, pushed past Joe and walked out.

"That went well, Joe."

Watching Arnholt disappear in the direction of the

ballroom, Joe faced his two club members, both grinning at him.

"I must say I've seen ram raiders with more tact," George commented.

Owen took the wind from his pal's sails. "About the same level you employed with Billy the kid this afternoon."

"Gar, get stuffed." George sank the rest of his pint, and cast an eye in the direction of Rose and Diane. "Tell you what, though but, if that dark haired little filly is a goer, she could have her wicked way with me tonight."

Following his example, Joe drained off his beer. "From all I've heard, you'll be at the back of the queue." He dropped the empty glass on the bar. "Better catch up with Sheila and Brenda. If Diane's interested in you, George, send her to me when you're through."

"You'll be no use to her by the time I'm done, Joe."

"I need a word with her, you banana."

He checked his watch and learned he had some time in hand before the band were due on stage. "Smoke, I think," he said to himself, and even the thought brought on a coughing fit.

It was no surprise to find Alec and Julia Staines taking up the smoke bench and enjoying the evening air. Julia did not smoke, but Alec did, and Joe often wondered how it was he'd been struck with COPD while Alec's had escaped it.

"For a start off, I don't smoke as many as you, and I don't roll my own. I buy low tar, tailor-made."

"And I make him go outside for a smoke when we're at home." Julia put on a look of sympathetic disapproval, leaving Joe to work out how anyone could achieve such a feat. "You really should stop again, Joe. Remember that heart-attack you never had? One of these days, it'll come knocking."

Joe settled himself on the end of the bench, next to Alec, and ignoring everything the couple had said, rolled a cigarette. "How did you get on with those cops, Julia?"

"No problem really. I think they were a bit miffed when I told them I hadn't renewed my nursing licence in God knows how many years, but like you said, someone had to do something for that poor man." She sighed. "And all to no avail."

"Murder's like that. We've seen enough of them in our time, haven't we?" Joe took a drag on his cigarette, suffered the inevitable bout of uncontrollable and unproductive coughing, and took a deep breath to settle himself.

Alec laughed. "Will you crack the case, Joe, before the ciggies get to you?"

Joe dug into his gilet, retrieved his inhaler and took a single puff. After holding his breath for the required five seconds, he let it out with an audible sigh. "I've never come across anything like this, Alec."

Julia disagreed. "Yes you have. You were just as bad in Windermere. You could hardly control—"

Joe interrupted. "I'm talking about Caswell's murder, not my smoking. I've been doing a little poking around for the cops, and this band are second to none. Bed hoppers unlimited. Everyone seems to be sleeping with everyone else… with the exception of the two gay men, and when you consider that the real target might have been Rose Louden, there are any number of potential suspects."

Alec laughed and Julia tutted.

"I thought some of them were married to each other." Julia's voice brimmed with disapproval.

"So they are," Joe said, "but they still like playing musical beds."

Alec stubbed out his cigarette and glanced at his watch. "Well, talking of the band, it's time we were getting inside. They'll be up and running in a few minutes."

Joe took out his phone. "I won't be long. I just want to make a quick call."

As they disappeared, he called up his phone's directory, picked up the entry for Yvonne Vallance and punched the connect button.

While he waited for an answer, he pictured the Palmer Hotel in his mind's eye.

A five-storey glass and concrete edifice, it could sit

comfortably amongst the office blocks of any town or city, without being noticed. It had no distinction, no character. Even the glowing, red neon sign and the pale cream walls of the front entrance said nothing about the building.

But it had its attraction. Behind the main building was a ramshackle shed, known as the old inn. In the dark, it was lit by sparse lamps, and weak bulbs on its walls, and had an air of foreboding about it. Built of stone, blackened by age, with a mock-Tudor front, it stood in complete isolation from the hotel and judging by the flat, empty fields all around the area, it appeared to have been ostracised from the rest of civilisation, too, and with typical Accomplus merchandising, it was reputed to be haunted.

Joe and the 3rd Age Club first came across it one Halloween, when they successfully cracked a couple of murders, and since then, he had spent occasional nights there, usually with his on/off girlfriend, Maddy Chester. When he was living with Denise, he had taken her there for Sunday lunch occasionally, and it was his proud boast that he had helped Yvonne and Geoff Vallance get together.

Yvonne was somewhere in her mid-forties, a good looking woman; slim, wide-eyed, a shower of pure blonde hair sweeping down over her shoulders, a full and proud bosom projecting above a slender waist, but she had a severely damaged hand, caused, so Joe understood, when she tried to drag her late husband from the ruins of a burning building. Vallance had been put off by that hand, and Yvonne herself was sometimes shy of it. Joe, it was, pointing out that there was more to attraction than the mere physical, and Yvonne was never slow to remind him whenever he visited the Palmer.

Someone picked up the phone at the other end of the call. "Palmer Hotel, Yvonne speaking."

A large grin spread across Joe's face as he answered. "Guess who."

She did not need to guess. "Joe Murray. How are you, you old toe rag?"

"All the better for hearing your sweet voice. And how are

you? Still married to Geoff and secretly lusting after me?"

"'Twas ever thus." She chuckled. "Hey, I had a query about you and your mob of born again teenagers last week. From Arnie Tunnicliffe at the Queen Elizabeth in Cleethorpes."

Joe frowned. "Tunnicliffe? He reckons his name is Turgot. Armand Turgot."

"And mine's Marilyn Monroe, but I'd rather be known as Yvonne Vallance." She laughed again. "He was always a snobby so and so. His name is Arnold Tunnicliffe, and he worked for me as a barman a good few years back. Hails from Gateshead originally. Started as a desk clerk straight from school, and worked his way up. Knows every aspect of the biz inside out. That's how come he was working behind the bar here."

"Yes, well, to listen to him, anyone would think he was educated at Eton and trained at Sandringham. He has so many plums in his voice, I could make a Christmas pudding from them. Anyway, we have more problems with him than his airs and graces."

"I've been hearing. One of the resident band was murdered or something."

"Poisoned. Household bleach in his cocktail. Turgot, Tunnicliffe, whatever you want to call him, was working behind the bar, and mixing the drinks, and he didn't get on too well with the victim."

Yvonne became serious. "If it was him, Joe, it was accidental. He's a pain in the buttock, but he's not malicious."

"Can't have been an accident, luv. The waitress dropped the first tray of drinks and he had to set them up again. If it was him, it was deliberate."

"I'm sorry, Joe, but you're barking at the wrong pussy cat. He has far too much to lose, and I don't just mean his freedom. He's spent almost thirty years climbing the greasy Accomplus pole, and if he was found to be spiking drinks, he'd not only lose his freedom but any chance of ever getting back into the hotel game again. I know that doesn't mean much to you, but knowing him, he'd have to have a serious life- or career-threatening grouse with the victim. Do you mind my asking, who was that victim?"

"Fella called Paul Caswell. He's—"

"A trombonist with the Shoreline Swingsters?"

"That's him. You know him?"

"We've had them here a couple of times, usually for weekend gigs. God, he was a pain. Hit on every woman in the place, including me."

Now Joe laughed. "If he was still here, I'd have him for that. He should have been told that when you've had enough of Geoff, you're mine."

"Carry on dreaming." There was a moment's pause. "Seriously, Joe, you should look at jealous husbands. He put it about like it was going out of fashion and he wanted to take his fill while he could. And he wasn't fazed, you know, when some woman – like me – told him where to shove it."

"Okay, kiddo. Unless you can think of anything, or anyone else, I'll leave it at that."

"Was he still jumping the band leader's missus?"

Joe laughed again. "You really did know him, didn't you? To answer you, yes, he was, and there's some suspicion that she might have been the real target."

Joe went on to explain how the drinks were mixed up and when he was through, Yvonne delivered her opinion.

"If anyone ever deserved throttling with bleach, it's her. Mind, I wouldn't go to the expense of a Tom Collins or even a spritzer. I'd have dropped the bleach into a glass of arsenic."

Joe laughed again. "Yvonne, you're a breath of fresh air."

"I'm pleased to hear it. When are you coming to see us again?"

"If you promise not to get all jealous, I'll bring my latest girlfriend over for lunch one Sunday."

"I think I can control the urge."

"Good. All I need now is a girlfriend. Are you busy next Sunday?"

# Chapter Twelve

Joe finished his cigarette and endured another bout of heavy, unproductive coughing, but this time he noticed a difference; a sharp, stabbing pain above the left breast, close to the point where his upper chest met his shoulder. The same pain he had felt earlier in the afternoon.

Today was not the first time, but with little to distract him, it was the first time that he was consciously aware of it, and the concern it brought. It brought back memories of Wes Staines' wedding in Windermere, and the severe coughing which led to the diagnosis of COPD. Within a few weeks, he woke one morning convinced he was having a heart attack. It wasn't, and after a week on the Costa del Sol, he felt much better. Yet the underlying truth about that improvement had less to do with the Spanish coast than with stopping smoking.

Taking a few deep breaths to ease the pain, he stepped back into the hotel. At once, his face spread into a broad smile when his eyes fell upon Armand Turgot busy briefing a member of staff at reception. Tuna fish, Caswell had called him, and in view of his real name, it was humorously apposite.

This, Joe decided, would be good for his chest.

When he approached, Turgot dismissed his assistant and gave Joe his immediate attention. "Can I help you, Mr Murray? Only I'm due on duty behind the ballroom bar in a few minutes."

"I've just had a chat with a mutual friend; Yvonne Vallance. She hasn't half told me some tales about you."

"I'm not interested in anything Mrs Vallance might have said."

"Well you should be… Mr Tunnicliffe."

Turgot's grim features betrayed no emotion, but his eyes narrowed a stare of daggers on Joe. "I don't have time for this."

"Then make time. Y'see, Inspector Gipton asked me to do some poking around. That's because there are restrictions on what the police can and can't ask. I don't have any such limitations, and when I bump into someone living under a false handle, I have to ask myself, what he's hiding."

"Then I'm sorry to disappoint you, but I'm hiding nothing. Now if you'll excuse me—"

Joe interrupted. "You've been told how Paul Caswell died?" He did not wait for an answer. "I was at the bar last night when you were mixing the band's drinks. It occurs to me that it would have been so easy for you to slip bleach into his Tom Collins, but Vicky dropped the tray, didn't she? And you were in such a hurry to replace the drinks that you put the stuff in the wrong glass."

Turgot strove to control his anger. "That is slander."

Joe looked around. There was no one else in reception. "You're right, it is slander, but only if anyone else hears it. It's not slander if I pass it on to Karen Gipton. It'll be a legitimate line of investigation for her."

"Well, let's hope she has more luck than you."

Turgot disappeared into the back office, and Joe walked into the ballroom.

It seemed to him that it was more crowded than the previous night, or perhaps it was because he was late arriving. He looked around, and spotted Brenda and Sheila at the same table they'd occupied on Friday evening, and he wove his way through the crowds to join them.

"Your beer's gone flat," Brenda announced. "Where have you been?"

"Making inquiries."

"And have you solved it?" Sheila asked.

"Some chance. I did have a nice little natter with our friend Yvonne Vallance nee Naylor, and she gave me some interesting information about old turbocharger. He's living under a false name."

Brenda pursed her lips. "And what's his real name, then? Aloysius Thorneycroft?"

Joe smiled. "Better than that. Arnold Tunnicliffe. Good old-fashioned Geordie name."

"You think he has something to hide?"

"Don't you?"

"Anyway, never mind the turbocharged Tunnicliffe. You've missed it all in here, Joe. It didn't half kick off."

"What did?"

Brenda took a slug of Campari, and licked her lips, ready to go into a lengthy explanation. "Too many people were harassing Alma about what's going on with Mort, and she lost it. I've never heard such language from a woman her age. Swearing like a trooper, she was. Mavis and Cyril tried to calm her down, and she turned on them. I tell you what, it's a good job she wasn't holding an axe. She'd have cut their heads off. She was like Boadicea charging a Roman phalanx."

Sheila picked up the tale. "Les tried to intervene and she gave him both barrels. Joe, we have to do something to track Mort down, and get him back here."

Joe shrugged. "I don't know what we're supposed to do. We need some clue as to where he is, and when I spoke to Alma… Yesterday, was it? Or was it this morning? I can't remember. When I spoke to her she as good as told me to mind my own business."

"It's getting to her," Brenda said. "She's just too stubborn and proud to admit it. If I get my hands on Mort, it won't be Les Tanner getting both barrels."

Joe sighed. "We're jumping to the obvious conclusion, but that's not to say that we're right. We haven't been able to speak to Mort to hear his side of the story, and until we do… Well, if you have any suggestions, I'm listening, but it's certainly putting the lid on what should have been a carefree weekend." He looked at his watch and read 8:25. "Anyway, what's up with the band? I thought they were supposed to start at eight?"

"The announcer came on half an hour ago and told us

they'd be late. They're probably still trying to alter the arrangements to account for Caswell."

Almost as Sheila finished talking, the lights dimmed, and the band began to take their places, while Rose Louden stepped into the middle of the dancefloor, microphone in hand.

"Ladies and gentlemen, the Shoreline Swingsters would like to apologise for the delay in this evening's entertainment. As you're all no doubt aware, our trombonist, Paul Caswell, died last night, and I'd like to ask you all to stand in a minute's silence, in memory of a man we, the band, knew well, and valued as a friend and colleague."

*And lover*. The thought jumped into Joe's mind as he got to his feet and clasped his hands. Unlike others, he did not bow his head, but instead, scanned the room looking for Alma Norris. There was no sign of her. Tanner and Sylvia Goodson sat to one side, on the edge of the dancefloor, and they had been joined by Alec and Julia Staines. Mavis and Cyril sat behind them, sharing a table with Norman and Irene Pyecock. Looking around the room, he could see other members of the 3rd Age Club, including Stuart Dalmer, a man Joe personally found annoying, but there was no trace of Alma or her wheelchair.

Had she sneaked past reception when he was speaking to Turgot? Or was she still in her room, contemplating the potential end of her marriage?

There was something about the scenario which did not quite ring true. He could understand her irritation with other members of the club. She was right when she told them to keep their noses out, and although he did not know her well, Joe was familiar enough to tell him that she was a tough old bird. The same could be said of many women from Sanford. But they were not invulnerable, and if it was true that Mort had another woman, Alma must be feeling the pain. And yet, she gave no indication of it. Her reaction was more in keeping with the 1960s theme of free love, 'tune in, turn on, drop out' than a diehard mining community in West Yorkshire.

His natural inquisitiveness would never let him drop the subject, but by the same token, he was wary of standing on delicate toes.

"Thank you, ladies and gentlemen."

Rose backed off to a position slightly ahead of her husband. He softly called time, and leaving Joe with a feeling of déjà vu, the band swung into *It Don't Mean a Thing (if it ain't got that swing)* the same number they had opened with the previous evening.

The whole repertoire was a repeat of Friday, and Joe noticed little difference until they played *Take the A Train*. His lack of musical knowledge aside, he guessed that Caswell's trombone, augmented by some of Heather's keyboard work, had contributed to the longer, deeper notes, a counterpoint to the intermittent, staccato beat of the trumpets, but without the trombone, Heather had to up her effort, while Tommy picked up the melody on the clarinet before Rose came in with the vocals.

It was impressive, and it raised Joe's opinion of them; a motley crew of questionable morals, they might be, but when it came to the music, they were professionals through and through.

The dancers took the floor, led again by stalwarts like Les Tanner and Sylvia Goodson. Sheila and Brenda joined in, Joe elected to sit it out, his thoughts whirling between the problems of Mort Norris's disappearance, Paul Caswell's, and how the band would cope for the rest of the season.

The latter, of course, was none of his concern other than the remote possibility that Caswell's murder had become the source of a cover-up for one member of the band, and that on the basis that while they could tolerate one missing trombone, to lose more instruments, particularly that belonging to the killer, would be a disaster, at least in the short term.

If that was the case it was a situation leaving them clinging to safety by the most fragile of threads. Louden said he could not replace Caswell at such short notice, but they were here until September and Joe had no doubt that a substitute trombonist would be brought in before long, but they were already in breach of the law; withholding evidence in a case of murder.

Could it be true? Could it be at the heart of the angry debate between Rose Louden and Diane Stott, the sulky silence of the Hollis couple, and were those sheets of music spread across the table no more than a cover for a more serious, criminal conspiracy?

With Sheila and Brenda dancing, he was mulling the idea when Vicky passed by and he ordered a fresh round of drinks. "They're keeping you busy, aren't they?"

"Too busy, Mr Murray, and Mr Turgot is cracking the whip like a slave driver."

Joe smiled by return. "If he gives you any real grief, tell him I know his real name." She laughed and was about to walk away, when Joe stopped her. "Just a minute, Vicky. You're permanent staff, aren't you? Some members of the band were here in January. Did you get to know them at all?"

Her ears coloured slightly. "Not really. They kept themselves to themselves. That Mr Caswell was a bit cheeky with some of us, but he was like that with everyone."

"So I've been told. All right, luv, you get back to your work, and remember if Turbo gives you any stick, let me know. I'll put him in his place."

He watched her wander off, the tray held high in one hand, zigzagging her way through the tables past others making for the bar, and he felt irritated for her. Turgot was a bully. No two ways about it. And what was it Yvonne told him about Caswell? *Hit on every woman in the hotel.*

"It's a different world, Joe," he muttered to himself as his friends came off the floor and the band called a brief intermission.

Sheila and Brenda were in high spirits, but Joe concentrated his eyes on Rose as she collared Vicky near the bandstand. Like the incident in the bar with Diane Stott, Joe could not hear a word, but he did not need to. The set of Rose's face, the way her chin jutted out, the frequent finger pointing were enough to tell him what was going on.

Vicky tried answering back, but Rose was not prepared to listen, and when she was through, she marched from the ballroom leaving the distressed waitress alone on the dancefloor.

"I'm just going for a smoke," he said to Sheila and Brenda.

"But Joe—"

"Later."

With Brenda furious at his departure, he left the ballroom and turned right towards the exit. He never left the room during the previous night's intermission, but having met Rose at the smoke area in the morning he knew he would find her there.

He was right. As he emerged and began to roll a cigarette she took a long pull on her smoke.

"Enjoying the show?"

"Not really my thing, this swing stuff. I was telling your old fella this morning, I'm more of a seventies man." He completed the cigarette and jammed it between his lips. "I'll tell you what I don't enjoy; watching you tearing a strip off the waitress. If you came into my café and harangued one of my staff like that, I'd throw you out."

"She's a gormless idiot. She was the one who mixed up the drinks last night."

"As a result of which you're still alive. You should be thanking her."

Rose glowered. "How many times have you been told to butt out and mind your own business?"

"As I said this morning, I don't think you could count that far."

She stood up, took another drag on her cigarette, deliberately blew the smoke in his face and dropped the cigarette to the ground where she crushed it underfoot. "You should be careful, pal. You're treading on toes which can crush you like an ant."

Joe stood his ground. "And you're looking at a man you can't intimidate… no matter how many fly sprays, lovers, and karate experts you bring with you."

She pushed her way past him, almost knocking him over, and Joe took the seat she had occupied, a fresh, more daunting possibility having just occurred to him.

The previous evening, he had seen Vicky point out the drink, but he had not noticed which glass Rose took. Suppose she, Rose, had spiked the spritzer and then deliberately taken the Tom Collins?

There were questions to be answered.

Motive first. Why would she want Caswell out of the way? Complicated but not impossible to work out. The affair turning sour, Caswell actually pleading Campbell Arnholt's case, Rose sick of Caswell's philandering (an old fashioned word but one which fitted Joe's frame of mind).

Next, how had she slipped the bleach into the spritzer? Again difficult, but not impossible. There was a confusion of events at the table when the band were collecting their drinks, and if she were quick enough, skilled enough at sleight of hand, she could have done it. And, of course, no one had been searched after the event. There was no need. Not until Caswell actually died, and that was hours later. Time enough for her to dispose of any evidence.

Finally, what was the little scene between Rose and Vicky about just now? Verisimilitude, that's what. Playing a game to distance herself from suspicion while attempting to lay part of the blame on the waitress.

But how would he go about proving it?

## Chapter Thirteen

"Joe, where the bloody hell have you been?"

Brenda's vehemence took Joe by surprise when he returned to the ballroom. "I went for a smoke. Why? What's the problem? You can't be that eager to dance with me."

"Who cares about dancing? It's you, Joe. Every time we turn round, you've disappeared for a smoke."

"I'm a smoker. It's what we do."

"Well, it's time you packed it in… again."

The incident with Rose and his suspicions following it had already ignited a slow-burning fuse, and Brenda's attitude fuelled it further. "Let me get this straight. The last time I checked – admittedly I can't remember when – this was still a free country. I don't owe you any more explanations for my smoking than you owe me for your shopping habits."

"Shopping doesn't kill you."

"Yes it does. It bores me to death."

Making an effort to pour oil on troubled waters, Sheila said, "We're concerned for your health, Joe."

"But not for my stress levels, obviously…" He trailed off on sight of Mavis Barker bearing down on them. "And if I'm not mistaken here comes another shedload of flak."

Mavis, a small, portly woman, barged her way through several people to get to their table. Her chubby face was bathed in sweat, and her features were set in a mask of fury. "Call yourself a bloody detective, Murray."

Joe felt his temper on the verge of exploding. "No. I call myself a caterer. I'm only a detective when it suits me."

"A waste of bloody space is what you are."

"Right. That's it. I'm—"

Sheila cut him off before he could snap. "Just a minute, Joe. Take a breath and calm down. The same goes for you, Mavis." She turned to the angry woman. "What's wrong now?"

"Alma has disappeared."

Sheila and Brenda were gobsmacked. Joe found his voice first. "What is this, the Queen Elizabeth Hotel or the Mary Celeste? How do you know she's disappeared?"

"Me and Cyril have just been to her room and she's not there."

Joe would not have it. "You mean she's not answering the door, and after what I heard of the way things went earlier, I don't blame her."

"She's… not… flaming… there, you dateless sod." Mavis jabbed the table between each word, causing the glasses to rattle. "When we couldn't get an answer we asked at reception and the kid on duty told us he saw her leaving the hotel."

"She's over twenty-one and she doesn't need anyone's permission."

"She's out there on her own." This time Mavis flung an arm out, indicating the great outdoors, and almost knocked Les Tanner off his feet. "Sorry, Les. I'm trying to get this idiot to listen to me."

"I wish you luck, Mavis," Tanner said and went on his way.

Mavis turned her anger on Joe once more. "What are you gonna do about it?"

"What do you suggest I do?"

"Get out there and find her instead of looking for the prat what killed the other prat. You're the club chairman aren't you? You're responsible for us."

Joe's temper finally gave way. "Wrong. I'm there to make sure you get on and off the bus all right, and that you get the rooms you paid for. I'm not a bleeding nursemaid, and if Alma has taken it on herself to go to the pub round the corner to get away from you, then good luck to her. Now do us all a favour, Mavis, and do an Alma. Clear off."

The volume of their exchanges had already attracted the attention of nearby tables, and Vicky made her way to stand close to Joe.

When she spoke, she was clearly nervous and embarrassed.

"I'm sorry, Mr Murray, but Mr Turgot has asked me to ask you to keep the noise down or please take your arguments outside."

"You tell Mr Tunnicliffe to get stuffed, and if you don't want to, I will."

Joe half rose before Sheila stopped him. "Stay where you are before you get us all thrown out." She smiled on Vicky. "Please offer Mr Turgot our apologies."

"Thank you, Mrs Riley."

While Vicky departed, Sheila concentrated on Mavis. "Is there anything to indicate that Alma has come to any harm?"

"She's on her own. She's stuck in that wheelchair. Isn't that enough?"

"Regardless, Joe is right, Mavis. Without a clue where to begin looking for her, we don't know where to start, and she was in a foul mood earlier."

Brenda chipped in for the first time. "And Mavis is right about him." She pointed at Joe. "He's too busy sucking up to the police and smoking himself to death to give a toss."

"And you can sod off, too." Joe stood up, dug out his wallet and threw a fiver on the table. "Get yourselves another round of drinks. I'll be outside… and no, I won't be looking for Alma Norris." He glowered at Brenda. "I'll be smoking myself to death."

He marched out of the ballroom and the hotel and flopped onto the bench by the entrance. The pain in his left, upper chest had returned, biting with every breath. Doing his best to ignore it, he rolled another cigarette, jammed it between his lips and lit up.

It was like pulling volcanic lava into his lungs, and the bout of coughing which followed did nothing to alleviate the pain. Instead, it aggravated it to the point where he began to wonder when or if it would expire, and what would be the outcome.

The memory of a rainy September morning invaded his mind. He was convinced that he was staring his own mortality in the face. He recalled the rising panic, the desperate phone call to Brenda, the nightmare ride in the ambulance, and the gradual easing of symptoms once the medics began to work on him.

He also recalled the doctor's words. "Pack the weed in or the heart attack you haven't had will happen."

Joe Murray was not, and never had been a coward, but he was no fool either. With some pressure from his friends, he took the doctor at his word and quit smoking.

But this pain did not feel the same. It was not spreading to either arm. It was a sharp stab to his upper left chest, and that worried him even more. For the umpteenth time, he checked the web on his smartphone, but finding the precise symptoms proved almost impossible. The moment he entered 'chest pain' into a search engine, the results concentrated on heart attack, and it did not matter how much he qualified the search, it brought the same results.

His gut feeling was that it had little or nothing to do with smoking, but the influx of tobacco aggravated whatever was wrong, but he knew that if he brought it up with his friends, he would get the same results as he did with the web.

He did not know how long he sat there smoking cigarette after cigarette. Les Tanner joined him once for a few minutes puffing contentedly on his pipe, and a little later, Alec Staines stepped out for a smoke. Both men were obviously aware of the earlier argument with Mavis, but neither of them mentioned it, and by unspoken, mutual consent, the subject of Mort and Alma Norris was taboo. Instead they talked about how they were enjoying the break and what a pleasant little resort Cleethorpes was.

Joe agreed with them even though he did not feel the same. In fact, he wished he'd never heard of Cleethorpes, he would prefer to be behind the counter of The Lazy Luncheonette or perhaps enjoying a drink with Alison in Playa de Las Américas, Tenerife.

Prompted by the thought, which came right out of nowhere, once he was alone again, he rang Alison, only to get her voicemail. He realised that she would be in the thick of the Saturday night throng in the Mother's Ruin, the popular Brit bar where she worked, and left a message asking if she could put up with him for a few days. She did not finish until turned one in the morning, and it would likely be lunchtime tomorrow before he got an answer.

Even as he rang off, he knew it was not a solution. Whatever flak he was coming under would still be here when he got back from the Canary Islands, and the annoyance of others would only be aggravated by his sudden disappearance. Believing him to be dead, they held a memorial service for him after he disappeared from Palmanova. If he pulled the same stunt again, the memorial service would be reserved for when he got back… after they beat him to death.

His watch read half past ten. He was still brooding on the confusion of arguments whirling round his head when a taxi pulled onto the hotel forecourt. The driver got out and lifted a small electric wheelchair from the boot, and Alma climbed from the rear seat and dropped into it.

Joe felt his anger rising again, and as if to remind him of his speculative conclusions, his left arm took a bite when he pulled on yet another cigarette.

The taxi drove away, Alma steered the wheelchair towards the bench and lit a cigarette. "Been looking for me?"

"Only me and half the civilised world."

She tutted. "When will you people learn?"

"They're concerned for you, Alma, and they're concerned for whatever Mort's up to. They don't want to see you hurt."

Her reaction surprised him. Not her dismissal of Mavis, Cyril, Les Tanner, other members of the club, and Joe himself, but the fury and street language she employed to deliver it. Both Sheila and Brenda had warned him, but even though he was no stranger to such basic curses – it was common amongst the Sanford draymen and other truckers – he did not expect to hear the same from a woman he had always considered well-educated.

And when the tirade ended, she rode roughshod over his efforts to explain.

"Any business between me and Mort stays with me and Mort. Now keep your bloody nose out. All of you."

Joe gave up the unequal battle. "In that case, Alma, you do

me a favour now, and get out of my sight."

She smiled. "Now that's more like Joe Murray." She took a long pull on her cigarette and Joe wondered how she could do so without the major coughing event to follow. "You know, you call yourself a detective. Truth is you can't detect what's right under your nose."

"And what's that supposed to mean."

"Instead of jumping on the tittle-tattle bandwagon, try thinking on what you know about me and Mort." And with that, she spun her chair round and made for the disabled ramp and disappeared into the hotel.

Joe puzzled over her final words. What did he know about Mort and Alma? It was not much.

They rented a two-bedroomed council flat off Leeds Road, not far from where Joe had lived after the old Lazy Luncheonette burned down. Mort was a permanent fixture on Sanford market and regular Sunday fleamarkets, Alma was from Wakefield and had worked in an office or something until she met Mort, moved to Sanford, and had a family, and afterwards she worked part time as a dinner lady in a Sanford school, and she stayed there for most of her working life until this last year when disability struck and she had to give up work altogether. As a couple they were staid, boring marrieds, never fussy, never over-demanding, never dealing in hopeless expectations. He understood that her diagnosis came as a shock to both, but like so many people in that situation, they adjusted, they coped. Mort was not given to tantrums or any form of temperamental outburst, and until a few minutes ago, Joe would have said that Alma was of a similar disposition.

All of which went to show just how little he knew of them, so how could that minimal knowledge tell him what was going on?

He was still turning the problem over in his mind when members of the band appeared from the side of the hotel, making their way to their respective vehicles, and Diane Stott made a beeline for him.

"If you spread any more vicious rumours about me and my

friends I'll go for you with a carving knife."

She was a slender, attractive woman probably in her early thirties. Slim, dark haired with a pretty, inverted pear-drop face, but as she ranted at him, Joe found her anything but appealing.

"Sod off." It was all he could think to say.

"And don't tell me to—"

The pressure of the evening snapped in Joe. He stood up and pointed at the band members. "If you want to talk about spreading rumours, missus, look at your pals here, not me. The only thing I'm interested in is who killed Paul Caswell… and my money is on one of you."

With that, Joe threw his cigarette to the ground, crushed it underfoot, and marched into the hotel. His left arm hurt.

***

Matters would deteriorate at breakfast on Sunday morning.

Joe had spent an uncomfortable, largely sleepless night. A couple of ibuprofen eased the pain, but he was constantly disturbed by a tight chest and an inability to cough up the rubbish clogging his airways. Every time he woke, the hassles of the day jumped into his mind and made it that much more difficult to get back to sleep. He finally gave up and got out of bed just after six. He showered and shaved and was wrapped in his coat and outside again by seven, enjoying his first smoke of the day.

Enjoying was the last word he would use to describe the violent cough and nagging pain in his arm and chest.

He returned to his room just before eight feeling exhausted and decided upon what was commonly known as a power nap. An inveterate early riser, fatigue, even at this level, did not normally trouble him. Behind the counter of The Lazy Luncheonette he was too busy to think about how tired he was.

The moment he hit the mattress, he was asleep and he woke at nine. Breakfast was calling.

Feeling slightly better, he made his way down to the

dining room, and at length joined Sheila and Brenda. Sheila asked how he was, he returned a taciturn grunt. Brenda did not speak to him.

But Mavis Barker did, and despite his attempts to ignore her and Sheila's to placate her, she laced into him with all the fury she had employed the previous night.

At length, his meal only half finished, he stood. "I've had enough." He glared at Mavis, then Brenda, then Sheila. "Of all of you."

He marched from the dining room, barely aware of Brenda following him. At reception, he hammered on the bell, and Turgot emerged from the rear office.

"Good morning, Mr Murray. What can I do for you?"

"I need to call a special meeting of my members. Give me the ballroom for an hour this afternoon. After the band have finished their session."

"We do not have conference facilities at this hotel, and even if we had, I don't know that I could arrange them at such short notice."

"Listen, smartarse, I am just about up to here with you and everyone else this weekend. Set something up or I get on the phone to Accomplus's Head Office and tell them how one of their managers is using a false handle in front of his guests. It may be nothing more than snobbery but I've been one of their best customers for years, and by the time I've done twisting the tale, you'll be on your way to London to explain yourself."

Turgot blanched. "Would four-thirty be all right?"

"Perfect." Joe turned and found Brenda standing behind him. He glowered. "Let the members know I've called a special meeting. Half past four, ballroom."

She had not spoken to him at all, but was about to say something. Before she could say a word, he stormed away and out of the hotel.

## Chapter Fourteen

He barely noticed the thin, Sunday morning traffic as he crossed the road and hurried through Pier Gardens making for Ross Castle. Once there, he followed the path which circled the lower bulk and led to the parapet.

It wasn't a proper castle. According to his research, carried out before they ever left Sanford, it was a folly, a tiny parody of a castle deliberately constructed as a ruin by some railway company back in 18-something-or-other. Built of rough stone, truncated, it was said that from the top, the view of Cleethorpes promenade and the pier was spectacular, and before he got there, he knew it would be no exaggeration.

Arriving at the top of the 'castle' he looked out across the choppy waters of the Humber Estuary. In the far distance he could make out the tiny tower of Spurn Point Lighthouse and recalled that he had never noticed it shining the night before. A minute or two of research on his smartphone revealed that although it was still there, it was no more than a tourist attraction. It had been deactivated and replaced by a beacon which flashed three times in rapid succession every five seconds. Joe supposed that modern navigation technology fitted to most ships, made the lighthouse redundant, and in many ways staring across the expanse of water, it mirrored his life. Maybe he could use some kind of navigational aid to mark out the direction he should take.

He was beset with problems. Crossing swords with Campbell Arnholt, Rose Louden, and Diane Stott, the arguments with Mavis, Alma's insistence that he mind his own business, and the vehement language with which she had delivered it, weighed heavily upon him.

Aside from a brief period when he handed over the reins

to Les Tanner, he had been Chair of the Sanford 3rd Age Club since its inception, and it was too much to expect an excursion to proceed without hitches, and murders were no exception, although they never involved club members… correction, they sometimes involved club members, but it never amounted to more than suspicion and it was usually Joe who put the police right. The odd member disappearing like Mort Norris was not unheard of, either. The treasure hunt in Whitby had seen Sheila AWOL for the whole weekend, and like Mort's absence, the members' general suspicion was that there was a man involved. It was almost absurd. Sheila had been a widow slightly longer than Brenda, and was utterly dedicated to the memory of her late husband. When the truth came out, it took everyone by surprise, and Joe was certain the same would be true of Mort's absence.

In the same way, the murder of Paul Caswell was an almost routine puzzle for Joe, and while he had always met with resistance from the potential suspects, he rarely encountered such ill-tempered obduracy as he had with Rose Louden and Diane Stott. When he did, it was on the assumption that they had something deeper to hide, and that only spurred him to greater effort.

And he did not mind. Without something like this to energise his hyperactive, inquisitive mind, he would spend the 3rd Age Club outings with Sheila and Brenda on their shopping expeditions. Shopping, he was always ready to admit, did not interest him. People did.

Right now, the twin problems were compounded by the inexplicable and worsening pain in his left arm and chest, and while it aggravated his irascibility, it was one he preferred not to discuss, even with his closest friends.

Watching the comings and goings along the seafront immediately below him, youngsters playing on the wide open sands, a couple of dogs gambolling in the shallow waters, their owners close by, he rolled and lit a cigarette, and on taking his first drag suffered an uncontrollable, coughing fit so violent it brought tears to his eyes.

Once again, it reminded him of that hot summer weekend

in Windermere when they had attended Wes Staines' wedding. That had been dogged by a murder, too, and it had been marred further by the state of his breathing. COPD was not the death sentence many people imagined, but it was incurable. Others smoked, some of them more than Joe, and he always considered it a bit of a lottery as to whether COPD struck or not. Hadn't he brought up the same subject with Alec Staines? Well, it struck him, and within weeks, he had stopped; given up the evil weed. And if he was honest, he felt better for it… until Palmanova when he started again.

To this day, he did not understand why. There was some crazy woman chasing him with intent to kill him, but taking up tobacco again did nothing to dissuade her. Neither did it alleviate his stress levels. If anything it made matters worse. Every time he stubbed out a cigarette, he wanted another and without it, he became fidgety and more irritable.

At the time, he told himself he was lucky; lucky that the damage did not seem to be getting any worse, but this weekend, with the sharp contrast between warm sunshine and a nippy wind, the number of problems laid at his feet as if he were some kind of messiah, he was smoking more and more, and he knew it could not go on.

Confronted with the discomfort worsening over the last twenty-four hours, many people would be panicked into concluding the onset of a heart attack, but it was not. It was too irregular and it did not fit the template of an MI. It was the gunge, the crap he took in with every drag on a cigarette, clogging up his airways, and no amount of strenuous coughing, no amount of assistance from his inhaler would shift it. If experience was anything to go by, he would need a course of antibiotics.

And he needed to make the effort a second time. Give up the tobacco before the chest pains really did herald a heart attack… or worse.

He had purposely refused to discuss the matter with Sheila or Brenda. They had been instrumental in compelling him to stop that last time, and he knew how determined they could be. He was often stubborn to the point of mule-headedness, but when they got the bit between their teeth, he could not hold a candle to them, and they were far less forgiving than his doctor.

He dug into his pockets, took out his inhaler and took two puffs, one after the other. It made him light-headed, but he knew it would help settle his breathing. And as if to pour scorn on his mental meanderings, he lit his cigarette again and took a deep drag. Better. No cough this time.

Soft footfall reached his ears. "I'm all right, Brenda."

"If you think I'm Brenda, you're anything but all right."

He turned to find Sheila coming towards him. "If I was a betting man, odds-on favourite would be Brenda," he said.

"And you would have lost. Brenda is very upset, Joe… with you."

"Now there's a surprise. She didn't say a bloody word all morning."

"And you didn't give her chance to say anything when she was with you at reception."

He turned back to gaze over the wall and out to sea where a passenger ferry plodded its slow way towards Hull, and Sheila stood alongside him.

"It's very peaceful here, isn't it?"

Joe waved an arm out at the estuary. "I've a pair of binoculars in my case. I bought them in Tenerife, if you remember. We could have had a lot better view with them."

"And is that why you came here, Joe? For the view?"

"No. I came here to get away from the rabble in the Queen Elizabeth Hotel, and you know it." He turned and fixed her eye with his. "Do you know what it's like when everyone wants a piece of you? They're like Jack Russell terriers. They won't let go."

"I worked in a school, remember, so yes, I know what it's like. But this is more than Alma Norris, Mavis Barker, and the Shoreline Swingsters, isn't it?" Sheila backed off from the wall. "My knees are aching because I came running after you. I know it's Sunday, but the cafes should be open, so why don't we go down to the front and find somewhere to sit?"

She turned away and retraced her steps following the

circular path around the faux castle. Joe stubbed out his cigarette, and followed. He had a shrewd idea what was coming, but trying to ignore it was like standing on railway tracks determined to ignore the express coming towards him. He could not complain. He was the same with them. When he needed them to listen, they would listen, no matter how reluctant they might be.

From Ross Castle they had to detour back the way they had come to the stone steps which would lead down to the promenade, and once there, they came to a small cafeteria/ice cream parlour, where Joe ordered two cups of tea, and they sat at an outside table, basking in the warm sunshine on the one hand, huddling into their coats against the chilly breeze on the other.

For all the comparatively early hour and the nip in the air, the seafront was quite busy. People, families of all ages, meandered along enjoying the expansive view, savouring an ice cream or a hotdog, and Joe assumed that like him, like Sheila, they were glad to be alive, glad to be out and about, glad to be in the pretty little resort. But Joe did not feel the necessary level of release.

Clicking two saccharine pills into her cup, Sheila sipped with approval, and spent a long moment staring out across the row, across the sands at the waters of the Humber and the low-lying landscape on the other side.

"If he were still with us, Peter would be in his element here. No stress, no worries, just the sun, the sand, and the sea." She focused on him. "A special meeting at half past four?"

"I'm quitting. The Chair, not the club."

Sheila sighed. "I swear there are times when you think Brenda and I are just fools."

There was no anger in her voice, no recrimination. It was simply a statement of fact and Joe chose not to respond, preferring to wait for what must follow.

"This business with the band, the death of Paul Caswell is getting to you. Every time you come across such a situation, you can't rest until you've cracked it. Mort Norris is playing some kind of game, Mavis and Cyril are worried about Alma's reaction to that game, and yet Alma is telling everyone to mind their own business and using some pretty choice language to get the message across. But asking you to keep your nose out is like asking a dog to guard the Sunday joint. And there's more to it, Joe, and I suspect that Brenda and I aren't the only ones who have noticed. You've been suffering some kind of pain for the last couple of days, and it's not just started. We noticed it at odd times in The Lazy Luncheonette and it's got worse since we got here."

Joe took out his tobacco tin and placed it on the table. It was deliberate and it provided Sheila with the perfect prompt.

She pointed an accusing finger at the tin. "Those things are the cause, but you already know that, don't you?"

He put the tin away again. "It's probably a fair assessment, but it's not strictly accurate. It's not just the smoking, Sheila. It's the whole thing this weekend: the band, Mort and Alma, Mavis – especially Mavis. It's driving me up the bloody wall and my answer to it is to smoke more and more and more. When we're in the café, there are restrictions. I've never been able to smoke in the kitchen, I never smoked in the dining room, other than when we took a break, and I can't do that these days. It's illegal. So when we're working, I pinch the odd five minutes for a smoke, but it's two, three, four times in a shift. This weekend, I'm almost chain-smoking, and yes I am getting some pain in my left chest and left arm, but it isn't a heart attack. I've done my homework and I think it's stress, and that's down to the hassle, the earache I'm getting, and the mouth I got from Mavis and Alma last night was the final straw."

"We guessed. After you left, when she came back from reception, Brenda told me what you'd said to Turgot and her, then she took Mavis to one side and gave her a dressing down. When you walked out just now, she was going to come after you – Brenda not Mavis – but I told her to stay put and I'd speak to you. When I left, she was looking for Alma, but I don't think it'll get her very far. You know what Alma's like. Skin as thick as a rhinoceros. A lot like you. And as for your pain caused by stress, I know it's possible, but I also know it's more likely to be heavy smoking." Sheila leaned forward, resting on her forearms. "You have a choice, Joe. You don't have to keep your eyes and ears open for the sake of the police, you don't have to report to them, you don't have to chase Mort Norris all over Cleethorpes and Grimsby, you don't have to put up with Alma's moods or Mavis's interference. You can say enough, I'm having a weekend off, and I'm going to enjoy myself."

Joe took out the tobacco tin again, and in a show of defiance began to roll a cigarette. "How? You know what I'm like. You know I can't back off from this Caswell business. He was murdered. Somebody has to pay for that."

"Yes, and it's up to the police to make them pay. Not Joe Murray."

"But I don't work like that, Sheila. That's what I said. It's a compulsion. I have to do it. The same applies to Mort. Alma said I should have realised what is going on, and for my money, he's found a bit on the side, probably with her blessing, and even though I told Mavis to go to hell, I agree with her. I think Alma's putting on a brave face, and somebody should collar Mort and tell him to grow up. But first we have to catch him."

The Lollipop Train drove past. A small tractor painted white, dressed up to look like an old-fashioned steam train, towing three small carriages, it was a popular attraction in Cleethorpes, and as it plodded its path, its three carriages full of passengers, many people on the sidewalks took out their cameras for a souvenir snapshot. Sheila made no apologies for being amongst that number, and it prompted a slight diversion during which Joe recalled taking a similar road train for a tour of Benidorm some years previously.

"The engine was a lot bigger," he concluded.

"And as I recall it had a much longer journey," Sheila said as she put her camera away. She drank more tea. "To shift the subject sideways, have you ever thought of becoming a professional private detective? I'm sure you could get a licence."

As if to demonstrate that he had indeed considered it, Joe lit his cigarette, suffered the inevitable cough, and said, "You don't need a licence to practice as a private investigator in the UK. It's odd when you consider the number of other walks of life where you do need a licence. Crikey, even to run the café, we need a hygiene certificate for every employee, don't we? But anyone can call themselves a private eye and charge for their services."

"There you are then."

Joe disagreed. "And what about The Lazy Luncheonette? What happens to that while Joe Murray is out there poking his nose into this that and the other? And it won't help with the stress, will it?"

Sheila pooh-poohed his objection. "After that business at Squires Lodge, you made Lee, Brenda and me partners in the business and insisted that you were going part-time. You never did. We could manage the café, especially if you take Kayleigh on. Besides, I don't know that there would be that many people in Sanford who needed the services of a private eye. You're good. You're one of the best. You shouldn't be doing it for free. You could even charge the police as a consultant."

For the first time since he left the dining room, Joe laughed. "Don Oughton would have a fit if I presented him with a bill."

Sheila smiled and tutted. "Still trying to evade the issue, eh? If you worked professionally, it would alleviate some of the stress for no other reason than you're getting paid, and that, in turn would help you with the smoking. And to labour the point, you really should stop smoking. You can do it. You did it before. Brenda and I will help."

"Nag the hell out of me, you mean."

She shrugged. "If that's what it takes."

Joe took another drag on his cigarette. "Brenda never said a word to me this morning, and all right, so I didn't give her the chance to say anything at reception, but then she tore a strip off Mavis. Why did she come out in support of her last night?"

"It's simple enough, and it's nothing to do with Caswell, Mort and Alma, or even Mavis. I lost my husband. Brenda lost her husband. Neither of us want to lose our best friend, and she's afraid that you'll be gone before your time. I'm worried about you too, Joe, but I tend to be less emotional about such things. Please, give up that evil habit." Once more, she pointed at his cigarette.

As if to show willing, Joe crushed out the smoke in the ashtray. "All right. I'll try. No guarantees, but I'll give it a go."

"That's more like… Mort."

"More like Mort?"

Joe followed her pointing finger, aimed towards the pier, several hundred yards distant. There was no mistaking Mort Norris's figure, shrouded in a topcoat, hurrying around the corner. From their previous day's outings, Joe knew that there was a steep hill round the corner, and at the top was the local bus terminus.

He finished his tea and stood up. "Let's get after him."

"We'll never make it."

"How do you know? You don't know what time the next bus leaves."

But Sheila was right. Several minutes later as they turned the corner, and stared up the hill, they could see Mort sitting at the rear of a single decker bus as it pulled away from the stop. When it came to the roundabout at the top of the hill, Mort looked back, saw Joe and Sheila, and gave them a two fingered salute.

## Chapter Fifteen

After checking the destination of the bus Mort had boarded, Joe and Sheila returned to the hotel, but on the way back, Sheila rang Brenda, and told her what they had seen. By the time they made the women's room, Brenda was dressed, ready to go, and it took only a few minutes for Joe to pick up the bits and pieces he would need… including his binoculars.

"Why are you taking those?" Brenda asked as they made their way back to the lobby.

"At least you're talking to me now."

"I was going to talk to you before, when you were hassling Turgot, but you didn't give me the chance."

"Serves you right."

"Whether or not, why are you taking binoculars if we're going to Grimsby looking for Mort?"

"In case he's signed on with a trawler and it's ready to sail."

"That sounds more like the old Joe," Sheila said. "The one we know and secretly adore. You're hoping we catch sight of him and his fancy piece from a distance?"

"Well, let's face it, he won't let us get close, will he?"

They left the hotel a few moments later, just in time to see a taxi, carrying Alma, drive away.

"Now she's gone," Brenda observed. "What the hell are those two playing at?"

"If we get a move on, we might find out when we get to Grimsby."

Joe always moved faster than the two women for no other reason than he was not distracted by shop windows, but as he walked ahead of them, he noticed that they were ignoring the few shops along the road, most of which were still closed anyway, and talking quietly between themselves. And without asking, he knew that he was the subject under discussion.

He felt a distant memory of peace descended upon him. Matters were put right, at least between the three of them. It was not uncommon for them to fall out with each other. He had been at loggerheads with Brenda in Cornwall, and again in Scarborough the previous Christmas, and both he and Brenda had been at odds with Sheila soon after her second marriage. It was a sign of true friendship that these disagreements, which were often quite serious, could be put right and the bond of friendship which had existed between them for half a century, re-established.

As they left the hotel and walked along the seafront towards the bus stops, Joe asked, "How did you get on with Alma, Brenda?"

"She told me to go forth and multiply, only her version was a good deal shorter and more to the point."

At the bus terminus, they climbed aboard, Joe paid the fare using his debit card – a move into the twenty-first century which he had not been aware of until the previous day – and he took a seat behind them, halfway along the bus. Five minutes later, the driver started the engine and pulled away, and almost immediately, Brenda moved to sit alongside him.

"Sheila's told me about your heart-to-heart on the seafront. If I was snapping at you last night, Joe, and ignoring you this morning, it had nothing to do with Paul Caswell or Mort and Alma Norris. It was all about you. You're not looking after yourself properly."

"I know that, but at the risk of starting another flame, it's down to me, isn't it?"

Brenda watched Cleethorpes town centre pass on the left, her brow furrowed, and he knew that she was calculating her answer.

"I'm scared, Joe. Frightened of losing you. I think Sheila is, too, but she won't admit it… Well, not in so many words." She paused a moment. "Do you remember how you felt when Denise was killed?"

He grunted. "Will I ever forget?"

"That's what I mean. Colin's been dead getting on for ten years. But I still remember what I went through watching him waste away. Now let me ask you another question. Do you think that only applies to husbands, partners? Don't you think it applies to best friends, too?"

Joe's wrapped an around her shoulder and hugged her. "After Lee, Danny, and maybe Gemma, you and Sheila are the closest thing I have to family, so don't think I don't appreciate your concern. Now can we concentrate on finding Mort and Alma?"

Brenda leaned across, kissed him on the cheek, and then returned to her seat next to Sheila.

A quarter of an hour later, they climbed off the bus near Freshney Place, and as always, the first port of call was the nearest café, where the women savoured a cup of coffee while Joe fed on a bacon roll and a cup of tea.

"Glutton," Brenda commented.

Joe was quick to defend himself. "I never managed to finish breakfast thanks to Mavis."

His remark gave Sheila the perfect opening. "And talking of Mavis, don't you think it's a bit extreme resigning the Chair, Joe?"

"I'm not resigning. I intend to resign, but I'm putting it to the members. They either give me a bit of breathing space or they put up with Les Tanner or, worse, Stewart Dalmer."

"Les was too busy crossing t's and dotting i's the last time he ran the club," Brenda said, "and if Stewart takes over, he'll use the position to push his business efforts."

"Well, who else?" Sheila asked. "Mort Norris, George Robson?"

Joe snorted. "Mort's skilled at sign language judging from what we saw earlier, and if you put George in charge, every excursion would be a brewery tour… or a visit to a brothel. I'm serious about this. Between Mavis and Alma, this weekend has been pure hell. The flak from the Shoreline Swingsters I could probably stand, but I don't see why I should put up with that kind of hassle… No, not hassle, abuse, from our members."

"I made that clear to Mavis this morning," Brenda told him. "Not sure if I got the message across, but if she gives you any more mouth, don't take her on. Leave it to me. Mind, to be fair to Mavis, she really is concerned for Alma. She's managed to persuade herself that Alma is suffering but putting on a hard front. What do you think, Joe?"

He did not need to think about it. "I think like Mavis, to some degree, but I also sympathise with Alma. It's none of our business."

"Then why are we here?"

Joe grinned. "To poke our nose in."

By the time they left the café, the town was coming alive. The area around the main shopping mall was crowded, the streets running at an angle and parallel to Freshney Place thronged with people taking advantage of the sunshine but wrapped up against the wind, and finding the proverbial needle in the haystack was child's play at the side of pinpointing Mort and Alma.

Inevitably, they wandered into the shopping mall, and before long the two women were engrossed in the goods on display. Joe left them to it, and went in search of another café where he could sit and mull over his thoughts, and soon he found himself enjoying a soft drink outside a small eatery opposite a well-known discount store.

He felt better. The pain of the last few days had receded to no more than a slight ache somewhere around his shoulder. He had made peace with his two best friends, Brenda had hopefully put Mavis in her place, Sheila had employed the usual policy of plain speaking, and her words made a lot of sense to him. Whether he would stop smoking or not, he could not say, but the act of bringing everything out into the open had brought a semblance of calm upon him.

It would not last long. Within a few minutes of taking his seat, Tommy and Rose Louden appeared at one of the entrances, spotted him, and made straight for him. From the look on their faces, he did not believe they were coming to congratulate him.

Rose towered over him and let rip. "You and your big mouth has practically wrecked our band."

Tommy nodded.

"Where the hell do you get off accusing one of us of murdering Paul?"

Once again, Tommy nodded.

The pain bit into Joe's chest and he took a deep breath to control it.

"We are innocent. D'you hear me? Innocent."

For the third time Tommy nodded in agreement with Rose.

Joe cleared his throat. "When did you lose your voice, Tommy? The day you married her?"

Rose appeared fit to burst, and Tommy spoke at last. "She's right, pal. You're wading in feet first, accusing the whole band of killing Paul."

"No. I'm accusing one of you. I don't know who, but your missus is favourite."

Rose opened her mouth to protest again, but Joe talked over her.

"I'm accusing the rest of you of knowing about it and covering it up for the sake of the band. I can't prove it, but I don't need to. The police will deal with that when I pass the message on. Whether you know it or not, concealing evidence of a crime, trying to bury it, aiding an offender, is a crime in itself, and the next thing you know, you lot could be entertaining the lags in the nearest prison."

"I've never been—"

Joe interrupted Rose yet again. "If you're going to say you've never been so insulted, then you ought to mix with more people. I'm on my way home tomorrow, but before I leave, I'll pass on every scrap of information, everything I've seen and heard, to DI Gipton, and if I have her sussed properly, she'll tear each and every one of you to pieces. Now do us all a favour and clear off."

Tommy found his voice again. "You're walking a dangerous line, Murray. Opening your mouth the way you do could get you a good kicking."

Joe took another deep breath and spread his hands. "Go

ahead. I'm on my own, and I'm well-known for my fighting skills... I don't have any. But do you think that'll change anything? Would you like to take me on when I'm with my members? George Robson and Owen Frickley, for instance? You think Arnholt's big. He's nothing at the side of them. Get this straight. I'm here for another twenty-four hours, and I will not go away. You want to see the back of me, then tell me the truth about Paul Caswell... and I don't mean his horizontal exercise habit."

Rose, determined to add the last word, stuck her nose in the air. "We'll be registering a complaint with Accomplus."

"Be my guest. Tell you what, do you want my business card so they know where to get in touch with me?"

Tommy scowled. "Bog off."

With that, the couple walked away, and Joe mentally congratulated himself. He had held his own against them, and if there was a downside, it was a return of the pain, but even that told him something.

It would be foolish to dismiss smoking as a factor, but the underlying cause was stress. Or maybe he had the two factors the wrong way round. The underlying cause was smoking, and the aggravating factor was stress. Either way, he needed to attend to both, and the sense of Sheila's words came back to him.

He could ring Karen Gipton and pass everything over to her, then ignore it. He could dismiss any passing interest in Mort and Alma. He could...

He trailed off as his mobile chirped for attention. He checked the menu window and read 'Alison'. He made the connection.

"Morning, girl. How's life in Tenerife?"

"Hot, sunny, and very relaxed, the same as always. The only downside is a voicemail from my ex-husband. Joe, what the hell's going on?"

"I'm sorry, Ali. I was a bit stressed out. Things are getting to me, and I shouldn't have called you, but the state I was in last night, it seemed like a good idea."

"You're poking your nose into things that don't concern

you again, aren't you?"

Joe laughed. "When do I do anything else?"

"Tell me about it."

Over the next few minutes, Joe gave her a brief rundown of the weekend's events, the murder of Paul Caswell, the mysterious disappearance of Mort Norris, and Alma's reaction to it. As always, his ex-wife listened, and it seemed strange to Joe. During the decline of their marriage, largely the fault of The Lazy Luncheonette, she had never been willing to listen to him.

When he was through, she pronounced judgement. "You never learn, do you, Joe? It's obvious to me that whatever's going on with Mort and Alma, it's private, so keep your nose out. And if you've got some brass band threatening you, the advice is the same. Mind your own. Finally, if you want to come to Tenerife for a few days, that's great, but give me a bit of notice so I can arrange time off from the Mother's Ruin."

Joe knew he would not accept the invitation, but he acquiesced all the same. "I'll do that. Look after yourself, Ali."

He cut the connection, settled back to enjoy his glass of lemonade, and as he did so, he caught sight of Mort, Alma, and a young blonde woman about fifty yards from him. He was about to get to his feet and approach them, when he stopped and stared in amazement.

Mort was talking, Alma and the young woman listening, and then without warning, the woman bent, and threw her arms around Alma, who responded by hugging the woman to her.

And in that moment, the truth – or, the apparent truth – occurred to Joe.

\*\*\*

Prior to facing the club members, Joe held a private meeting with Les Tanner and Stewart Dalmer, Sheila and Brenda, and after about thirty minutes, having spelled out the situation and his intentions, they moved from the bar to the ballroom, where Joe confronted the rest of the members, minus Mort Norris and his wife.

He had said nothing to Sheila or Brenda on what he had seen in Freshney Place. Indeed, he was still trying to put together a working theory, one that did not encompass extramarital mischief on Mort's part. It wasn't difficult to see the truth, but he knew too little about Alma for him to reach an accurate conclusion. Whatever the outcome, Alison had called it right from two thousand miles away, and Mort and Alma had been hinting, albeit not so gently, at privacy all weekend.

That could wait. For the moment, he intended bringing the members up to speed on his position.

With Sheila taking the minutes, he stood before the group and opened with an apology.

"I'm sorry for calling you together while we're on what's supposed to be a weekend away, but as I'm sure you're all aware, things have got a little out of hand over the last twenty-four hours."

Mavis stood up and raised her hand. Joe raised his eyebrows, inviting her to say whatever she had to say.

"I'm sorry to interrupt, Joe, but it's been made clear to me what a pain I've been since Friday, and I owe you a personal apology. To be fair to myself, I am seriously concerned for Alma, but I was a bit over the top."

Joe smiled. "Thank you, Mavis. The only thing I can suggest is take more water with it in future." His remark provoked a ripple of laughter. "All right, now that we've heard from Mavis, I'll ask you all to listen to me. This weekend, you've driven me up the bloody wall. Not just you lot, granted, but in combination with other things, you have driven me bananas, I have to consider whether it's worth going on as Chair of the Sanford 3rd Age Club. Right now, I'm considering my options, and leaning towards resigning. I've spoken to Les and Stewart, and both of them are happy to stand in an election." He turned from the crowd. "Sheila?"

She got to her feet. "With Mort and Alma absent, there are

not enough members here for a quorum, so whatever decisions are made, they'll have to be ratified at another meeting."

"Thanks, Sheila," Joe said, and concentrated once again on the members. "I'm calling for opinions."

Alec Staines got to his feet. "No disrespect to Les or Stewart, Joe, but neither Julia nor I want to see you go. As far as we're concerned, you're the best man for the job."

Alec sat down, George Robson stood. "I'm with Alec. I'm not knocking you, Les, but when you took over before, it wasn't the same. We can't rag you the way we do Joe."

Over the next few minutes, there was a consensus of opinion that persuaded Joe in favour of staying where he was.

He took front and centre again. "All right. I already know Les and Stewart's opinions, but it's up to them to divulge them if they wish. But I wanna make one thing clear. When we're away, if you have any problems, by all means come to me with them, but cut me some slack. I can't always help myself from poking my nose into this and that—"

"Not to mention the other," George Robson chipped in.

"That's your forte, George, not mine. I was saying, I can't always help myself, but let's all learn to back off a little bit. And if no one else has anything to say, that's it."

The meeting began to break up, and Sheila applauded Joe. "Very tactful."

Brenda agreed. "It was. Totally out of character."

Joe smiled. "I keep telling you, I'm full of surprises."

## Chapter Sixteen

It was a much more contented Joe who joined his two companions for dinner that evening. He felt relaxed, almost free of pain, and glad to be in the company of people he had known for most of his life, people he considered friends.

He was no closer to solving the murder of Paul Caswell, and if he had a hint to explain the mysterious behaviour of Mort and Alma Norris, it was with a feeling that he would never get to know the truth, but he had rationalised both problems, and if he was only 'almost' free of pain, the residual twinges were the result of his smoking not stress. In deference to Sheila and Brenda's insistence, he had cut back, but he had not yet stopped, and the tobacco still caused him some grief.

After the club meeting, he returned to his room and rang Karen Gipton to inform her that although he had not arrived at a satisfactory solution to Caswell's death, he had a series of observations for her, and he promised to email them to her before the Sanford party left Cleethorpes the following day.

He remained convinced that Caswell had been poisoned by one of his colleagues, but it would be, "Hell's teeth of a job to prove it, especially the way they close ranks."

It was after speaking to her that he realised how little contact he had had with the police since Saturday. On other occasions, he had been hand in glove with them for most of the inquiries, and that was true even for those investigating officers who did not want him there.

The visit to Grimsby and concomitant later return to the hotel meant they missed lunch, but to their delight, they learned that the traditional Sunday roast beef and Yorkshire pudding, was still on the menu, and while Sheila and Brenda chose to share a half bottle of house red, Joe washed down his meal with a half of lager.

The intervening three hours had seen many of the club members approach him individually, most of them asking him to stay as Chair of the 3rd Age Club. He remained non-committal, but privately, he had already confided in his friends that he would not step down.

Mavis Barker found him enjoying a smoke outside at six o'clock, and apologised personally to him while maintaining her insistent concerns for Mort and Alma. Joe reassured her that her angry outbursts would be consigned to the realms of the best forgotten, and they parted as friendly as they had ever been.

After dinner, he made his way outside once again to enjoy another smoke, and was joined by Alec Staines and Les Tanner. As with the previous evening, they tactfully steered the conversation away from the weekend's problems, and instead concentrated on the positive aspects, one of which was how pleasant they had found Cleethorpes and its surrounding environment.

Employing his new-found diplomacy, Joe agreed, and declared that one of these days, he would return to the town – probably alone – to take in more of the North Lincolnshire area.

In the bar before they came onstage, the Shoreline Swingsters gave him plenty of mutinous stares, but none of them approached him, and some time after eight o'clock, they took to the stage, and with the same raw enthusiasm they had portrayed on the previous evenings, ran into a repeat of their repertoire. This time Joe did not wait until he was sufficiently drunk before taking both Sheila and Brenda – one at a time – to the dancefloor.

During the interval, he stepped outside for a cigarette and a minute later found Heather Hollis sat alongside him. Of the band, she, her husband, Nigel, and Freddie Brackley were the only members he had not spoken to, and he was surprised to find her, if not pleasant, then at least reasonable.

"I'm not going to plead with you or threaten you, Mr Murray, because from all I've seen, it's a waste of time."

"It is. I'm sorry, lass, but I don't like murder, and whoever did this should answer for it. And I don't care how much of a lothario Caswell was, he didn't deserve to die."

"You're right on both counts. My concern is your insistence that the band are coming together to protect the guilty. It's not so... well, let me correct that. I can't speak for the others, but Nigel and I are not party to any conspiracy."

Joe laughed. "And I have your word on that, do I? See, according to the two star-crossed lovers, Billy and Ed, you're a married woman who was happy to jump Caswell while your husband was servicing Diane. How reliable does that make either of you?"

Her ears coloured. "I can see why my colleagues are critical of you."

"Because I tell it like it is, you mean? Well, let me tell you something else. There are two main contenders for the murder; Rose Louden and you. Rose because she might have had enough of him, and you because the poison was aimed at Rose, and if she's out of the way, you're top vocalist."

She laughed. "Is that what you think? Or have you been listening to more of Ed and Billy's gossip? Let me tell you something, Murray. I don't like this band. I don't want to be in it. They don't play our kinda music, but it's all Nigel and I could get when we came back to England."

Joe frowned. "Came back?"

"We were working a string of bars in the Puerto del Carmen area of Lanzarote. Just me and Nige. Carpenter lookalikes and we did a lot of their music. You must have heard of the Carpenters."

"I'm old enough to remember them for real. He played the joanna, his sister was a drummer."

"Yes, well I play keyboards, and Nigel is a good, all-rounder. He plays piano and guitar as well as trumpet and sax. We were good, but I got homesick." She laughed again. "Can you imagine that? Homesick for this sad, cold little island."

Joe shrugged. "I felt the same way when my ex-wife asked me to ship in with her in Tenerife. I couldn't do it. I like this sad, cold little island."

"Yes, well, all we could get was session work with Tommy and his band. Me take over from Rose? To sing that crap? She can have it. She might have choked Paul, she might have got fed up of him, but it wasn't anything to do with me."

And with that, she flounced off the bench and back into the hotel.

Joe took this jaundiced view back into the ballroom where he joined Sheila and Brenda and related the incident to them.

"What impresses me is their professionalism," Sheila said. "You watch them perform and you wouldn't think there was any argument between them, and yet, in private, they're quite happy to tear one another to pieces."

"I think most performers are like that," Brenda said. "Remember Skegness and that silly performance of Hamlet. While they were on stage, they were brilliant – comical script aside – but offstage they didn't have an awful lot of time for their leader, did they?"

The final question was aimed at Joe who was not listening. Instead he was watching Vicky wandering through the tables, delivering drinks, leaving bills, loading the empty tray with glasses and bottles. The girl looked absolutely worn out, and it caused him to wonder just how hard Turgot worked his staff. Ambition was one thing. Trying to achieve it on the back of others' exhaustion was an entirely different matter and he resolved to register a complaint with the Accomplus group.

But it was not enough to put him off enjoying himself for once, and throughout the second set he danced, or sat tapping his feet, drumming his fingers on the table in time to the beat. He had already resigned himself to his failure in the murder of Paul Caswell, and managed to push it to the back of his mind, along with the troubling twosome, Mort and Alma Norris.

At eleven o'clock, they enjoyed a final nightcap, and made their way back to their rooms. Sheila unlocked the door of the women's room and disappeared inside. Joe turned to bid Brenda 'good night' but before he could utter a word, she pressed him into his room, followed him, and closed the door behind her.

"I owe you an apology, Joe Murray, and if I have to, I'll spend all night apologising."

\*\*\*

It was a revitalised man who rolled out of bed at half past seven the following morning. Brenda was still asleep alongside him, and as always, he was in need of a cigarette.

He showered, shaved, dressed and made his way down to the lobby and out to the front of the hotel, where he basked in the early, chilly sunshine, lit a cigarette, did his best to ignore the coughing, and relaxed.

Keith would pick them up in less than seven hours, and two hours beyond that, they would be back in that small mining town east of Leeds, southwest of York, the place they called home. He was not looking forward to it, but accepted it as part and parcel of life. What was it someone once said to him? If you didn't have the downside, how would you know when you were enjoying the upside?

On reflection, it had been a poor weekend, but the last fifteen hours, eight of them spent in Brenda's vigorous and demanding company, would put a pleasant seal on it, and before too long, he would forget the bad in preference to the good. It was the way of life.

Tomorrow he would call his doctor, and beyond that, somewhere along the line, he would make a stronger effort to live without the evil of tobacco. Later in the year… Well, nothing had been decided on future excursions, but no doubt someone would come up with an idea.

At eight o'clock, he made his way into the dining room and joined Sheila and Brenda for breakfast. Some members of the 3rd Age Club were already there, and while they worked their way through a two course meal, cereal and milk followed by a full English complete with tea and toast, more of their party drifted in. As always, George and Owen looks slightly worse for wear, and Joe guessed that they had been out drinking again on Sunday evening. Tanner was already dressed in grey trousers and his regimental blazer, and matching tie, ready for the journey home. The Staineses too were dressed for the two-hour journey.

Once breakfast was over, they made their way back to their rooms, and Joe decided against changing his clothing, and cleared out the bathroom, throwing his shaving gear and minimal cosmetics into his small suitcase. He raided the wardrobe, taking down the clothing he had not worn, folded it more carefully into the case before zipping it up, ready for vacating the room.

He had the puzzle of his newly bought model trawler and how to get it safely from Cleethorpes to Sanford. Eventually, he decided to leave it in the giant carrier bag in which it came, and stow the same in the luggage rack above his seat. At least that way, he could look out for it.

With the time coming up to half-past nine, he made a final check of the room, happy that he had taken everything belonging to him and none of the hotel's property, and made his way to the ground floor where he handed the key to Turgot.

The manager, imperious as ever, thanked him. "I hope you've enjoyed your stay, Mr Murray."

"I haven't, and to be frank, you haven't made it any more pleasant. It remains to be seen whether I'll take up your attitude with your bosses."

Turgot sneered. "I'm sorry about that, but you'll forgive me if I say I really don't give a damn."

"Where can we leave the luggage until the coach arrives?"

"There's room in the bar. As long as you and your members keep it all together in one corner, you can collect it when your transport turns up."

Joe made his way into the bar and found a whole bunch of suitcases of various sizes squeezed into a corner. He left his there, and carefully placed his model trawler on top of it. He then crossed the room to join Sheila and Brenda with the intention of asking them if they fancied a final walk round Cleethorpes, but Sheila's concern beat him.

"It's Mort and Alma, Joe. Here we are ready for going home, and they've disappeared again."

## Chapter Seventeen

Joe crossed the room again and dug into his suitcase. A moment later he came out with his binoculars. "Keith is due to collect us in a few hours, so it's a safe bet that wherever Alma is, it won't be far. Let's see if we can find her, huh?"

"And what about Mort?"

"If my suspicions are correct, he'll be with her."

With him leading the way, they left the hotel, crossed the road and made their way through Pier Gardens, but instead of heading down to the seafront, Joe branched off into Ross Castle.

Sheila and Joe had seen the view, and while Brenda marvelled in the spectacle, Joe checked the distant view of Spurn Point and its tiny lighthouse, clearly visible through the lens of his glasses, and the shipping moving to and fro along the Humber Estuary, before concentrating his mind and bringing his focus closer and scanning the promenade, sweeping the lenses slowly along its length towards the pier and beyond.

"Can't see any sign of her wheelchair."

He turned his attention in the opposite direction, but once again drew a blank.

He chewed his lip. "She could be anywhere."

"The pier?" Sheila asked.

Joe trained his glasses along the short pier and beneath, and shook his head. "Nothing."

"Why don't we take a walk along the seafront?" Brenda suggested. "You never know, she might be hiding, keeping out of the way. If she's suicidal—"

"I'll eat my hat… and yours, and I'll take Sheila's for afters."

Joe's cynical interruption did not sit well with either of the women.

"What do you know that we don't?"

"Nothing, I'm just putting it together better than either of you."

"Well, stop being a smartarse and let's get moving." Brenda turned on her heels and led the way from the castle, down onto the seafront where they turned left and walked towards the pier a quarter of a mile distant.

The sun had shone all weekend, and this day was no exception. The sky was bright and cloudless, but the chill wind which had troubled them since Friday still nipped at the cheeks and ears.

None of them had any mind for the discomfort. Their eyes were everywhere looking for a tell-tale sign of Alma or her electric wheelchair.

It was Sheila who spotted it, parked outside a café opposite the pier. "All that adrenaline for nothing. She decided to go out for a cup of tea."

"She's probably sick of Mavis Barker winding her up." Joe checked his watch. "Quarter past ten. Keith is due at two o'clock. What say we join Alma for a brew and a bun and a heart-to-heart?"

The women agreed and he led the way across the road, but when they stepped into the café, there was a surprise for the two women, but a triumph for Joe.

Alma was there, so was Mort, as Joe had predicted, and between them sat the blonde woman they had seen with Mort on Saturday morning and Joe had seen with both Mort and Alma on Sunday.

Mort groaned. "Joe, why can't you—"

"Shut it. You two have made a hell of a mess of my weekend, and it's time you brought us up to speed." Joe stared at Alma. "Especially you."

While Sheila and Brenda gathered chairs around the table, Joe went to the counter and secured tea for all six, and a selection of cakes. After paying for them, he, too, joined the group.

"This is not exactly a turn up for the book, Mort. We saw you with this young lass on Saturday, and I saw the three of you in Freshney Place yesterday. Everyone has drawn the obvious conclusion, but after what Alma said to me the other night about the answer being right under my nose, I figured that arranging for your mistress to meet with your wife is a bit strong."

Mort scowled. "Bog off, Joe. All of you. Alma's been telling you all to mind your own bloody business since Friday."

Joe held up his hands in surrender. "And I've been telling Mavis and Cyril to mind it, but they've badgered the hell out of us." He turned to Alma. "Don't you think you owe us some kind of explanation?"

"No, I don't. But I will, if only to shut you up." Alma smiled. "Joe, Sheila, Brenda, let me introduce you to Robyn Kinsey. Robyn, this is Joe Murray, Sheila Riley, and Brenda Jump, three of the nosiest buggers in Sanford."

They nodded a greeting to the woman and she responded with a thin smile. The counter hand brought half a dozen beakers of tea and a plateful of cakes, and cleared away the empty cups, and while she did so, Joe assessed Robyn.

He judged her to be about forty years of age. An attractive woman, clad in a fashionable, tightfitting jumper which had the effect of exaggerating her bosom, her blonde hair hung in long, straight lines, framing a pretty face which bore a small mouth, lips pursed in what might be concern or disdain, and blue eyes which Joe thought could be expected to sparkle, but yet, there was a hint of... something about them. Sadness? Worry? Annoyance? It defied analysis, and they could only wait for Alma, Mort, or indeed, Robyn, to explain the complex situation.

On the other hand, the convivial placidity between the three, led Joe to conclude that his friends, and indeed the whole of the 3rd Age Club had been ploughing the wrong furrow, and that his assumptions from the early hours of the morning were more accurate..

No one was say anything, so Joe led. "It's a pleasure to

meet you, Robyn, but you really don't want to know what the rest of our members are saying about you."

"They can say what they want, Mr Murray. Alma, Mort, and I know the truth."

Her accent was North Lincolnshire. If pushed, Joe could never pinpoint the difference between it and the accent of Hull, which was flatter than the more familiar South Yorkshire of Doncaster, but lacked the broader intonation of Lincoln and all points south. Whatever it was, it was not West Yorkshire.

He concentrated on a minor point. "Please call me Joe. It is my name, and I have been called worse, especially by Sheila and Brenda, and your Aunt Alma."

"Only because you deserve... Aunt Alma?" With this exclamation, Brenda turned her attention to Alma. "You're her aunt?" She fumed. "Everyone in the club is worried about you. We know that it's not our business, but that's the 3rd Age Club, isn't it? We look out for each other, and we were concerned that you were hiding your pain. Now you tell us this is your niece?"

Alma laughed. "You don't half talk some twaddle." She eyed Joe. "Especially you. Listen to me, all of you, I know where Mort's been all weekend, and I know what he's been doing, and before your one track minds wander off on the wrong spur, Joe is half right. Mort hasn't been sleeping with Robyn. He's dossed at her house this last couple of nights, but not in her bed. I think her husband might have objected, don't you?"

Joe suspicions took the final twist, and with an insight often delivered to most people, the truth dawned on him.

"How old were you when Robyn was born, Alma?"

Sheila and Brenda gaped again. Mort fumed, Robyn's eyes opened wide, but Alma laughed.

"A lot of people tell me you're the best detective in Sanford, Joe. I always had my doubts, but credit where it's due, you've got there at last. Taken you long enough, but you've finally rumbled it."

Robyn focused her attention on Alma. "He's a detective?"

"He's a nosy so-and-so, luv, but according to those in the know, he's solved more crimes than Sherlock Holmes." Alma faced Joe. "To answer your question, I was barely sixteen years old. I'm from Wakefield, as you know, and Robyn was the result of a chance encounter with a kid on a fairground. A bit of rough-and-tumble in the woods behind the rugby ground, and nine months later, Robyn turned up."

Brenda was speechless. Mort reached a hand across the table and took Alma's, and Robyn took a napkin and dabbed at her eyes.

Sheila was more practical. "This was at a time when such things still mattered, wasn't it?"

"It was. Back then, a young girl like me getting herself pregnant brought shame on the family. Pah. What utter nonsense. But I had no option. I had to give Robyn up for adoption. Life went on. I eventually met and married Mort, and we had our own family, but I never forgot that little girl I held in my arms for a few minutes on the night she was born."

"You knew about this, Mort?"

In response to Joe's question, Mort's irritation rose. "Course I bloody knew. We've no secrets from one another, me and Alma. I knew before we was married, but we kept it to ourselves. Why shouldn't we? It was nothing to do with anyone but us."

Brenda emerged from her stupor. "You're right, Mort, but I'm surprised the Sanford grapevine never cottoned on."

Alma agreed. "But I don't come from Sanford, Brenda. Besides, even if anyone knew, it would have been forgotten over the years."

Joe made an effort to bring the discussion up-to-date. "So what happened? You knew of your adoption, didn't you, Robyn? And you made an effort to find your real mother?"

"Right on both counts, Mr Murray."

Joe sighed. "Joe. Please."

"As you wish, Joe. It took me a while to track Alma down, and when I did, I wrote to her. Can you understand what it's like, learning that the parents who brought you up were not your real mother and father? You'd never believe what I went through: sadness, joy, relief, and downright anger. At its worst, I seriously resented Alma for giving me away. Not that I had a bad life. My adoptive parents brought me up well. I wanted for nothing… other than to know who my real mother was. And then, Alma replied, suggesting we meet."

A lightbulb lit in Brenda's head. "Cleethorpes. You were the one who pushed for it, Mort."

He shrugged. "Alma persuaded me, and it seemed like the best idea. We're staying in Cleethorpes, Robyn lives in Grimsby, what better way for the adopted child and real mother to meet?"

"So which one of you was frightened?" Joe asked. "I don't believe it was you, Alma, so it had to be you, Robyn, didn't it?"

The adopted daughter nodded. "I still didn't know how I felt. There was still some anger at the way I had been… well, abandoned, I suppose, from my point of view. So I arranged to meet with Mort, not Alma, and he's been with me, my husband, and my two kids for most of the weekend."

"And he's been reporting back to me," Alma added. "If you'd been that good a husband, Joe, maybe Alison wouldn't have cleared off to Tenerife."

"If he'd been that good a husband, I'd have snapped him up years ago," Brenda said.

The light-hearted remark relieved some of the tension, and Sheila directed the next question at Robyn.

"Why wait until yesterday? To meet Alma, I mean? Why meet Mort but not Alma."

The younger woman shrugged. "My fault again, Mrs Riley. I was nervous. Frightened, even. Mort and my old man spent most of Friday and Saturday persuading me that I should meet with my real mum. I finally found the courage yesterday, and that's when you saw us, Joe."

"And today's the last meeting for a while," Mort put in. "We're on our way home at two o'clock. Robyn's husband dropped us here at nine, and Alma turned up ten minutes later."

Now Alma took Robyn's hand. "We've had a weep, we've exchange photographs, Robyn's children, my two, and I explained the situation as it was when Robyn was born. To be honest, Joe, Sheila, Brenda, I was ashamed of myself back then. I should have insisted on keeping her."

Sheila shook her head. "You were sixteen years old, Alma. At that age, we know everything about the world, but the truth is, we know nothing. We only think we know. Even if your parents were prepared to support you, life would have been hell." She transferred her gaze to Robyn. "I assume you know nothing about Wakefield or Sanford, so you may not appreciate what I mean."

"I think I do, Mrs Riley. The housing estate where I grew up is rife with exactly the same, small-minded attitude. I've seen many a girl tarred with the 'whore' brush for making the same mistake Alma made, and some of them were younger than Alma was when she fell on for me."

Joe sipped from his beaker. "People call me a miserable old sod, and maybe they're right, but you know, I always try to think of the future, not the past."

Chewing through a cream bun, Brenda chuckled. "Take no notice. He's more old-fashioned than Mort and Alma."

"Bog off, you. What I'm trying to get at is, what's the way forward for you?"

Alma sighed. "We're on our way back to Sanford this afternoon, and Mort will be on his stall tomorrow morning."

"But Ian – that's my husband – and I will be taking the kids to Sanford over Easter so they can meet their third grandma." Robyn smiled on Mort. "And their other grandad… again."

Brenda applauded, Sheila smiled, and Joe sat back, satisfied with the outcome of one of the two puzzles which had nagged him all weekend, and it was he who posed the final question.

"So who's going to tell the club members?"

Alma laughed again, a hint of mischief in her eyes. "They can do like I say and mind their own damned business. That Sanford grapevine will do the job when Robyn and her family come to visit."

It was coming up to half past ten when Joe, Sheila and Brenda left the newly found family to themselves and stepped out into the morning sunshine.

As they did so, Brenda glanced down at her dark pants, now stained with cream. "Blast. I was going home in these. I'll have to go back to the hotel, open my case and change."

"It's only a bit of cream, dear. If you sponge it out, I'm sure no one will notice."

"I'll know," Brenda retorted, licking the corner of a handkerchief and rubbing at the stain.

"Turgot might, too. I had to tell…" A shock of realisation ran through Joe. "Oh, my god. That's it. I've been barking up the wrong tree all weekend." He took out his phone and dialled Karen Gipton. While waiting for her to pick up, he said to his friends, "We need to get back to the Queen Elizabeth, sharpish… Karen? Joe Murray. Listen, I know who did it. Get yourself and Watney to the hotel and all will be revealed."

## Chapter Eighteen

Three quarters of an hour later, having been briefed by Joe, Karen had all the members of the band, Turgot and Vicky Ordish gathered together in the ballroom, and the air was thick with rumblings of discontent, much of it coming from the hotel manager.

At Karen's insistence, Joe, with Sheila and Brenda seated behind him, took centre stage, and for a long moment, he said nothing, but scanned the assembled group with a disapproving eye. Finally, he went into his analysis.

"I have a reputation as a private detective second to none. Very little gets past me, but to look at me you wouldn't think so, and I find that useful. You all look down your noses at this quirky, grumpy little man from West Yorkshire, and you think, 'what a berk'. I can deal with that because it means you will say things to me that you wouldn't say to your average police officer, like Inspector Gipton. You think it all goes over my head, and you're wrong. It all sinks in, and somewhere along the line, you trip yourself up."

Once more he scanned the line of people facing him, seeking signs of discomfort. Not yet. He hadn't begun to pinpoint the tiny hints which had led him to his conclusion.

"I remember Cleethorpes from when I was a kid, and even then I thought it was a singularly boring little town. Thanks to you lot, this weekend has proved me wrong... well, I suppose the place is still small and insignificant, but it's more than can be said for you people. Like me, you're all nobodies, unlike me, you all have dreams of grandeur, and it reflects in your – to me – outrageous behaviour. Shoreline Swingsters? You should think about renaming yourself Bed-Hoppers Anonymous. In my time, I've come across a fair number of people jumping into beds they shouldn't be, but as far as I can recall, this is the first time I've met with serial adultery confined to such a small group of people, and when Paul Caswell died on Friday night, it automatically pointed the finger at most of you. And Paul, rest in peace, was one of the worst. He'd jumped all three women in the band, so it was natural to assume that when he was poisoned, it was either one of those women or one of you men who'd had enough of his shenanigans. When it became obvious that he picked up the wrong drink, that it was the spritzer not the Tom Collins which had been spiked, we automatically assumed that the real target was Rose, and that brought more suspects into play, particularly Heather, the second vocalist, Diane, who has a wonderful time with Rose's husband, Tommy, and you, Campbell, because you're short of money and Rose controls it."

Arnholt interrupted. "I told you, you were talking out of your backside, and I told you that if you open your trap much more, I'll close it permanently."

Joe dismissed the complaint with a downward sweep of his hand. "Try insulting my steak and kidney pudding and you might worry me." He returned to addressing everyone. "When I remembered Rose talking to Vicky on Friday night, and then saw her remonstrating with the same kid on Saturday, it automatically suggested Rose as a suspect. Had she spiked the spritzer and then deliberately picked up the Tom Collins, then argued with Vicky to mislead me?"

Rose responded with a vehemence equal to Arnholt's. "I did nothing of the kind." She aimed an accusing finger at Vicky. "This silly bitch got the drinks mixed up."

Joe smiled. "Did she? We'll have to see about that." He faced the hotel manager. "There was at least one other suspect; you, Turgot. You're a snob, and we all know of your arguments with the band, particularly Paul Caswell."

"I don't have to answer that allegation."

"Somewhere along the line, you may have to. Not long after we arrived, you badmouthed my good friend Yvonne Vallance, and as I told you earlier, I rang her, she told me all about Arnold Tunnicliffe, a snooty kid from Gateshead with ideas above his station."

"How I choose to lead my life, and what name I choose to go under, is no concern of yours or the police's, as long as I'm not trying to profit by deceit. I'm employed by Accomplus under my real name, but I choose to use Armand Turgot when I'm on duty."

"Yes, and Paul Caswell knew about that, didn't he? I heard him refer to you as tuna fish, and I couldn't understand it. Not until Yvonne told me your real name. And on Friday night, you were behind the bar mixing the drinks. You pointed out to Vicky which was the Tom Collins and which was the spritzer. It was busy at that bar, and the two drinks did look alike, so how do we know that you weren't telling her the wrong way round?"

"I refute that. It's not my fault if this stupid girl doesn't know the difference."

Joe's eyes lit up. "Ah, now there you've hit on something. I have a nephew, Lee. He's a smashing lad." Joe settled his eyes on Arnholt. "Twice your size, and if he was here, and you threatened me, he'd make mincemeat of you. He doesn't have a malicious bone in his body, but he's a big clumsy so-and-so. He's cost me a fortune in broken plates and wasted food, but he's a brilliant chef. There is no meal he can't prepare and produce. He's like an idiot savant, a great, gormless sod, but in his own way, he's a genius. We also employ a young girl, Kayleigh Watson, and she's the same. Both of them are valuable employees, and I wouldn't be without them despite the trouble they cause me. So I was caused to wonder why you keep Vicky on if she is so bad? I narrowed it down to only one conclusion; you're sleeping with her."

The announcement created an immediate furore from Turgot and Vicky, both vehement in their denials.

Joe ignored it. "It also occurred to me that if someone like Paul Caswell made a pass at her – let's be honest, it was his forte – you'd be a bit irked, and that would be motive enough for you to spike his drink."

Turgot got to his feet. "I deny it. And I deny that I'm sleeping with this woman. I won't listen to one more word of this." He stood and marched towards the ballroom exit, only to find his way blocked by Sergeant Watney, who silently invited him to return to his seat.

Joe pressed on. "I said at the outset that nothing escapes me, and that includes Vicky's alleged poor performance. Before that incident on Friday night, I noticed her waiting on tables in the ballroom. She was brilliant. No matter how many full or empty glasses it had on it, no matter how tired she was, she carried the tray in one hand, and delivered the drinks perfectly. After a tiny, silly incident this morning when my friend, Brenda, spilled cream on her dark trousers, I was caused to wonder how Vicky managed to drop the tray after leaving the bar on Friday night. On Saturday, I had occasion to speak to her on the whereabouts of a personal friend – it's all right, Turgot, she told me nothing so she didn't breach your idiot privacy rules – and she was brushing down her skirt. I never thought any more about it, and she laughed it off as muck and dust, and she'd clean it up before her boss saw it. But you never did, did you, Vicky? Because it wasn't muck and dust, was it?" His eyes narrowed upon her. "It was a bleach burn, and you picked it up when you dropped the first tray, and you dropped that because you were trying to pour bleach into the glass while you were weaving your way through the tables. Isn't that right, Vicky?"

The colour drained from her shocked face.

Joe pressed on. "You managed it second time of asking, but you dropped it into the wrong glass. You put it in the spritzer instead of the Tom Collins. Or was that deliberate? Did you deliberately mix them up and then made sure that Caswell would get the wrong glass? That way, you knew it would lead us to conclude that Rose was the target – or the suspect – but she wasn't. Was she?"

Without warning, Vicky burst into tears, burying her face in her hands. Watney made a move towards her, but Joe held up a hand to stop the sergeant. "Give her a minute."

Eventually, Vicky emerged from behind her hands. "I

didn't mean to kill him," she wept. "I was only trying to make him ill."

Joe nodded to Karen, who indicated that everyone should leave but for Joe, Sheila, Brenda herself, and her sergeant.

All accusing eyes turned towards Vicky, the band filed out, followed by Turgot.

Joe, his two friends, and Karen drew their seats near to Vicky. Sergeant Watney stood behind the distraught girl.

Sheila took her hand. "Tell us what it was all about, Vicky. Trust me, you'll feel so much better if you bring it all out in the open."

Brenda passed Vicky a tissue, the young woman dabbed at her eyes. When she looked at them, it was an appeal for their understanding.

"He used me. He came here in January with Tommy and Rose. They were booked for the season, and they came to check the hotel out. They spent three days here, and he had me every night."

Brenda was shocked. "Are you saying he forced himself upon you?"

"No. No. Nothing like that." Vicky shook her head. "I was happy to go with him, Mrs Jump, and he fed me the usual line about how attractive I was, how good I was to him, and how much he was looking forward to the season when he and I could get together more often."

Joe understood. "But when he turned up, he was more interested in Rose, Diane, and Heather, wasn't he?"

Vicky nodded. "The first day they were here, I went to see him at the Sunbeam Guest House. I waited across the road. There's a bench where you can sit."

"I sat there too. That's where I saw him and Rose."

Vicky responded directly to Joe's announcement. "Yes, well, I saw him with Diane, and it didn't take a genius to work out what they were doing. When he came to the hotel, I met with him, and he told me to… Well, I can't repeat it because I don't use that kind of language, but I was determined to get my own back. Friday night was the perfect opportunity. The ballroom was full, I was waiting on tables, and I had a small bottle of bleach in my pocket. You were right, Mr Murray, I deliberately mixed the drinks up. I was sure no one saw me dropping the bleach in the spritzer, but when I put the glasses down, I pointed to the Tom Collins, and told Rose that that was her drink. She didn't question it." Vicky's features twisted into a derisive sneer. "That woman is no better than a snooty tart. She wouldn't pay much attention to a lowlife like me. But the minute she took a drink while she was singing, she knew I'd got it wrong. I don't know how I kept from laughing." Once again she pleaded with them. "But I didn't mean to kill Paul. I just wanted to make him ill, pay him back for the way he used me and then dropped me."

She began to cry again and Sheila patted the back of her hand.

When she looked up, Vicky concentrated upon Karen. "Will I go to prison for a long time?"

"That will be up to the judge, Vicky, not me. I have to bring charges against you. If we can get some corroboration of most of your story, I'll try to press for manslaughter rather than murder, but it will be up to the Crown Prosecution Service, the Department of Justice or whoever. No matter what charges I'm going to bring, I have to arrest you, and take you to the station."

Joe bristled. "I'm sorry, Vicky, but I don't accept that Caswell deserved it. That's the way I am. I always think everyone has a right to live long enough to learn from their mistakes. What I will say is that he was scum, and you had a right to be angry with him. But there were better ways of dealing with it. There's any number of magazines out there, and any number of websites, where you could have exposed him as a philanderer, or love rat, or whatever they call such men these days."

Vicky was not persuaded. "If I'd done that, Mr Turgot would have sacked me for bringing the hotel into disrepute."

Joe snorted. "You shouldn't be worrying about tosspots like Turgot, either. He's a class conscious snob."

Brenda agreed. "To be honest, Vicky, although you didn't

know it, your best course of action would have been to speak to us. We have a friend who works for Accomplus. Yvonne Vallance runs the Palmer Hotel near York, and I'm sure Joe could have persuaded her to spill the beans on Arnold Tunnicliffe, and we could have railroaded Paul Caswell for you."

Karen stood up. "Victoria Ordish, I'm arresting you on suspicion of the murder of Paul Caswell. I must caution you that you do not have to say anything, but if you fail to mention something…"

With more than a hint of sadness, Joe, Sheila and Brenda left the ballroom.

\*\*\*

"That poor girl."

It was gone twelve noon. Keith would turn up in a couple of hours, and they were taking a final stroll along the promenade, pausing occasionally to look over the vast spread of the Humber Estuary as they made their way towards the pier.

Silence was the order of the day and had been since they walked out of the Queen Elizabeth, each immersed in their own thoughts, until Brenda's comment broke into them.

"You mean Vicky?" Joe asked.

"Who else?"

Brenda stopped, leaned on the rail and looked out over the sands, watching the gulls circling, landing, feeding, their ever-hungry eyes alert for the possibilities.

Joe and Sheila joined her, and she looked from one to the other. "She was right about Caswell. He used her. It's guys like him who give you men a bad name."

"I agree. I said the same about Chew in Scarborough, but like Chew, Caswell didn't deserve to die. He should have been made to face up to his behaviour, grow up, learn that using, abusing women like that is wrong." He took out his tobacco tin, caught a frown from Sheila, and changed his mind. "Do we believe Vicky when she said she didn't mean to kill him? I think I do."

Sheila was in no doubt. "I'm certain of it. What was it you said about Lee? He doesn't have a malicious bone in his body? I think the same applies to Vicky. She was hurt, she was angry, and I think she just wanted to teach him a lesson. And if she needs a character witness in court, I'll be there."

Brenda sighed again. "Can we put it all aside, and concentrate on the journey home? We've hardly seen anything of Cleethorpes. Just this little bit and the main shopping street. I'm sure there's a lot more to the place."

"Quite a bit," Joe agreed as they began walking towards the pier again. He pointed behind them. "There's a big leisure centre and a massive boating lake about a mile that way. And there's a massive holiday park about another mile further on."

Brenda chuckled. "How do you know? You said you haven't been here since you were a kid."

Joe held up his smartphone. "Internet on the go. This piece of tackle is not just for reading e-books, you know."

They moved further on. Across the road, opposite the pier, Mort, Alma and Robyn looked as if they were making ready to part company. Sheila and Brenda gave them a wave as they passed and turned into the pier.

They walked into the café they had visited on the first day, and while Joe secured drinks and snacks, Sheila and Brenda sat by the windows, looking out on the bright, sunny day.

"On your way home, are you?" the assistant asked.

"Another couple of hours."

"Did you catch the tide?"

Joe scored her a point for her memory. "Too busy, luv. I've promised myself that I'll make a point of looking for it the next time I'm here."

"Well, I hope that won't be long."

He joined his friends at the table.

"Have you made a decision about Kayleigh, Joe?" Sheila asked.

"Yes. But I'm not gonna tell you what it is."

"Have you made an appointment with your GP?" Brenda demanded.

"Not yet. Let me get back to Sanford." He held up his hands in a gesture of innocence. "Come on, give me a break. I promise I'll deal with it, and I will."

"Good. So all's right in the world."

Sheila did not quite agree. "Yes, but I'm not sure that Vicky Ordish thinks so."

## Chapter Nineteen

Dr Ahmed Khalil made a note of the blood pressure readings, and removed the cuff from Joe's left arm.

Joe waited, watching his GP transfer the readings to his computerised records, then switching screens to made more notes before hitting the 'enter' key and sending a prescription to the printer.

The virtual nightmare that was Cleethorpes lay over a week in the past, and Joe had been true to his word. He had not stopped smoking, but with Sheila and Brenda keeping a wary eye on him, he had cut down dramatically. Those same women had insisted he make an appointment to see his GP, and he had reluctantly agreed. With the time coming up to ten o'clock on Tuesday morning, he was in a hurry to get back to the café, but Khalil seemed determined to take his time.

While the laser printer processed the instruction, turning out a standard NHS prescription form, Khalil clasped his large hands across his distended belly.

"Right, Joe, I suspect the main cause of your problems is stress aggravating your breathing difficulties. I've prescribed a new inhaler. It's a steroid. Medical name, beclometasone dipropionate, but you can call it your steroid inhaler. You use it twice a day. Two puffs first thing on a morning, two puffs of an evening every evening, and you'll probably find you need to swill your mouth with salt and water after using it. Make sure you always have your Ventolin inhaler to hand. The steroid is a long-term treatment, but it's not a quick reliever."

Khalil reached behind him, picked up the prescription and Joe reached out a hand to take it. "Thanks, Doc. I'll—"

"Not so fast, my man. I haven't done reading you the riot

act yet. It's all very well saying your breathing's aggravated by stress, but it's also aggravated by smoking, and don't pretend you've given it up. I know different. I could smell the tobacco on you when you came into the surgery. Now listen to me, my friend, because I'm being serious. If you don't give it up, Sheila, Brenda, and young Lee will be having a proper knees up very soon... At your funeral. We know it's not easy, but if it helps, I can get you counselling."

Joe pulled a face. "I'd rather not, Doc. You sent me to a smoking counsellor once before, and we got so far down the line when he suggested trying a prescription designed to suppress the cravings. Well, I'd had it before, and I had a bad reaction to it. You know what he said when I told him that? He said, 'not to worry, we'll give it a try'. As I understand it, part and parcel of counselling is listening as well as talking, and he didn't want to listen."

Khalil shrugged. "Then the only option open to you is cold turkey. Do you think you can do it?"

Joe's reply was hesitant. "I did it before, with help from Sheila and Brenda. You've never seen two people like them. Once they get the bit between their teeth, they're like Rottweilers."

"In that case, stop dithering, and get on with it. I don't see much of you, thank the Lord, and to be honest, Joe, the less I see of you the happier I am, and that's not just because you're a grumbling old so-and-so." With a smile, Khalil handed him the prescription.

An hour later, clutching his new inhaler, Joe walked in through the rear door of The Lazy Luncheonette to be greeted with concerned anticipation from his friends.

"Well?" Brenda asked.

"Bloody fool should be struck off. Tells me it's stress then tells me to stop smoking. Smoking helps me cope with the stress. And I told him, I said, I wouldn't have any stress if it wasn't for you two."

Brenda screwed up a serviette and threw it at him. "If you think you're getting away with it that easy, Joe Murray, you've another think coming."

Sheila concurred. "We'll help you, Joe."

"That's what I told him. He's prescribed a new inhaler. A steroid. I know about them. Will it give me muscles like Schwarzenegger, do you think?"

Brenda grinned. "You already have the same muscles as Schwarzenegger. It's just that you tend to hide them under your whites."

Sheila laughed. "Joe, you're thinking of anabolic steroids."

"And anabolics to you, too." He took a seat across the aisle from them, and called into the kitchen where Lee, Cheryl and Kayleigh were busy preparing lunches. "Kayleigh, do me a favour, luv. Get me a cup of tea, and come and sit here for a minute."

Sheila and Brenda exchanged knowing glances. Kayleigh, on the other hand, appeared distinctly wary when she carried a beaker of tea to the table, and sat facing him.

He dug into his pocket and came out with a small set of documents, which he pushed across the table to her. "This Thursday and Friday, Sanford Technical College, hygiene certificate. It's compulsory, luv. You can't carry on working here without one… Especially now that we're making you permanent."

Sheila and Brenda cheered, and in the kitchen, Cheryl and Lee actually applauded.

"It's a good college, Kayleigh," Lee encouraged her. "I went there for years."

Joe smiled. "It took them three years to find out how thick he was."

Kayleigh was close to tears. "Oh, thank you, Mr Murray. I don't know how to thank you."

"You just did. Now that you're onside, there are a couple of rules to working here, Kayleigh, and the first is you stop calling me Mr Murray. My name is Joe."

"But I can't do that. It's not respectable."

"You mean respectful. I don't mind, Kayleigh."

She thought about it for a moment. "Can I call you Uncle Joe like what Lee does?"

"You can call me Uncle Zebedee if you prefer, as long as it's not Mr Murray."

Kayleigh looked over her shoulder. "Did you hear that, Cheryl, Lee? I can call him Uncle Zebedee."

Joe closed his eyes and shook his head. "There's another rule, Kayleigh. You keep away from the barista machine until you've been properly trained in using it. I don't want any more cappuccinos made with fruit yoghurt."

Kayleigh agreed, but across the aisle, Brenda cocked her head to one side as if considering the proposition. "How about cappuccinos made with plain yoghurt?"

# THE END

# The STAC Mystery series:

#1 The Filey Connection
#2 The I-Spy Murders
#3 A Halloween Homicide
#4 A Murder for Christmas
#5 Murder at the Murder Mystery Weekend
#6 My Deadly Valentine
#7 The Chocolate Egg Murders
#8 The Summer Wedding Murder
#9 Costa del Murder
#10 Christmas Crackers
#11 Death in Distribution
#12 A Killing in the Family
#13 A Theatrical Murder
#14 Trial by Fire
#15 Peril in Palmanova
#16 The Squire's Lodge Murders
#17 Murder at the Treasure Hunt
#18 A Cornish Killing
#19 Merry Murders Everyone
#20 A Tangle in Tenerife
#21 Tis The Season To Be Murdered
#22 Confusion in Cleethorpes
#23 Murder on the Movie Set

Tales from the Lazy Luncheonette Casebook

**By the same author:**

#1 A Case of Missing on Midthorpe
#2 A Case of Bloodshed in Benidorm

#1 The Anagramist
#2 The Frame

# Fantastic Books
# Great Authors

darkstroke is
an imprint of
Crooked Cat Books

- Gripping Thrillers
- Cosy Mysteries
- Romantic Chick-Lit
- Fascinating Historicals
- Exciting Fantasy
- Young Adult
- Non-Fiction

Discover us online
**www.darkstroke.com**

Find us on instagram:
**www.instagram.com/darkstrokebooks**

Printed in Great Britain
by Amazon